REVIEWS

"You should put something in the title to alert citizens
that this book will cause severe paranoia. Seriously."
—Todd "Semen" Niemen

"Oh, man. I don't know whether the stuff you said is true,
but if it is, then I'm pretty much freaking out right now."
—Zach Tuggs

"What did I just say?"
—Todd "Semen" Niemen

GHOSTS/ALIENS

Three Rivers Press
New York

GHOSTS/ALIENS

Trey Hamburger
(Robert's cousin)

Published in the United States by Three Rivers Press, an imprint of the Crown Publishing Group, a division of Random House, Inc., New York.
www.crownpublishing.com

Three Rivers Press and the Tugboat design are registered trademarks of Random House, Inc.

Library of Congress Cataloging-in-Publication Data

Hamburger, Trey.
Ghosts/aliens / by Trey Hamburger.—1st ed.
p. cm.
I. Title.
PS3608.A5499G48 2008
813'.6—dc22   2008017404

ISBN 978-0-307-40730-6

Printed in the United States of America

Design by Maria Elias

All interior illustrations courtesy of Worawalan Chantawong

1 3 5 7 9 10 8 6 4 2

First Edition

You are about to become aware of the unknown—or at least something only a couple dudes know.

LEGAL NOTE

i.) OK, I hate to have to say this kind of thing, but the law requires that I must. If you have one of the names used in the book, and I DON'T personally know you, then I wasn't talking about you, and *any resemblance is purely coincidental.* But if I DO know you personally, and, for example, I call you retarded, then it wasn't coincidental, and you probably are retarded.

ii.) If you accidentally invoke a demon or open a portal and weird shit starts happening, Trey Hamburger, Mike Stevens, and the people we hang out with are NOT LIABLE.

iii.) This book contains a lot of profanity and salty language. Some of it very intense—but it's the only way to get across how freaked out we are.

C O N T E N T S

Tell the Scientists of Planet Earth, *Don't Be a Dick*   xvii

Derek sees something weird   4

He gets upset   4

He calls me about it   4

I get upset   7

Mike and I think about how this kind of thing happens a lot *and nobody does a thing*   8

Mike and I get pissed   8

Outline my new scientific role in life   8-9

Prepare people for the shit I will say   11

Say it   12

Warn people about ghosts   13-15

Try getting some scientists to tell us the truth   19

I go over to Derek's house to investigate what he saw   21

Feel weird about it   22

See something   24

Then just start running   24

Examine what we found   25

Relax   25

But then see some dude doing something messed up, and hear a noise   26

Freak out   26

Scientist replies to our letter   27

We get pissed about it   28

Send him a reply back   28

Something big happens to an amigo   38

Jeff Trenton freaks out and tells us about it   39

Mike and I freak out   40

Then Jeff asks for a burrito   40

We don't give him one   40

Later, we tell some professor about what happened to our amigo   41

He doesn't care   42

We hear some weird-ass noise   43

And start watching the neighbor   44

Study broadsword techniques   46

City council denies request to attack neighbor   49

Sneak into some dude's house   54

See some messed-up shit   54

Run   55

Celebrate and reflect   55

Recover from seeing some messed-up shit   57

Try to get some funding   59

Study ghost/alien weaknesses   61

Don't get any funding   66

Get pissed   67

Think about dead amigo   69

Get pissed about it   70

Catch a really old guy   71

Dude just starts puking   71

Ask him a bunch of questions   73

Then have a really messed-up experience   74

Feel weird about that   75

Then get mad (most mad so far)   76

Mike gets pissed   76

Make a really intense decision   77

Warn people about messing with this kind of stuff   78

Discuss space/time intricacies   81

Mike's cousin tells us some major shit   87

Feel a lot better about life   89

Then I clear my name after somebody starts saying shit   90

Mike and I decide to fulfill some prophecy   91

Make a blood pact   91

Get pumped about that decision   92

Slap five hard   92

Start an Elite Fighting Force of Dudes   93

Try to get NASA involved   95

They don't care   96

We get pissed   96

Mike calls them *buttholes*   96

A bunch of weird shit starts happening down the street   97

We start keeping watch   98

See some messed-up shit   99

Mike and I discuss combat techniques   100

Get pumped about our Fighting Force   106

Try getting a local militia in on it   110

They won't   111

Mike and I talk to some people and hear some more
messed-up shit   114

Feel weird about it   114

Go home   114

Decide to train our psychic powers   115
Consider letting poultry join the team   120
Mike is hesitant   121
Test our powers   122
Get pissed   124

Discover some majestic shit   125
Get pumped about it   127
Talk to some more dudes, hear some more weird shit   132
Mike just starts shaking   132

We consult a warlock   136
And then regret it   137

Later we decide to link our brains together   140
Talk about Einstein's latter years (weird)   140
Try to get funding for experiments   144
Nobody wants to help out   145
Get pissed again   148

Mike and I think about life and start freaking out   149
Wonder if our thoughts are really our own . . .   152
We finalize our conjectures before we go on a major trip   157

Attack neighbor   161
It backfires   164
Decide to go on the trip anyway   167
Get pumped about it   169
Try to get some dude to come with us   174
He won't   175
We get depressed   176
Mike tells an inspirational story about a guy with
rabbit feet   176
Feel better   177

Write our wills   180

Try to leave for our voyage   183

Can't   184

Get pissed   184

Mike and I make an epic voyage   187

But realize we messed up big time   193

And start wiggin' out   194

Still wiggin' out   195

Mike and I stop wiggin' out   197

And try to get Nobel Prizes   203

Find out some bullshit   207

Get pissed   209

Think about the meaning of life   211

Feel better   214

Don't get any Nobel Prizes   215

Get even more pissed   217

Go fight some being   218

Duck helps out   221

Discover the unknown   223

Get pissed one last time   225

Chill   230

EXHIBITS AND SECRETS

History of the potato chip   232

Proof I would never eat a certain shaped cracker   233

Top-secret document   234

Alien abduction test   235

Suggested workout schedule   236

How to start your own Force   237

Letter to CERN   240

Letter to Nabisco   242

Letter to some dude   243

EFFD initiation   245

NFRP certificate   246

Support groups   247

Investigation Notes I   248

Investigation Notes II   249

Dear Scientists of Planet Earth,

The following text may be the most important written in the last couple centuries, and could be compared to the Copernical Revolution. In its totality, it comprises a body of evidence so profound that it will numb the human experience beyond comprehension.

On Friday, Mike Stevens and I discovered some major shit. And we definitely think you guys should know about it. Don't worry, I wouldn't be contacting you unless I was totally sure. Which I am. So far, we talked to everybody we know and THEY don't even know what to say. So hopefully, you people can help out because I got some highly classified information that you guys should be probably telling all your coworkers.[1]

For a long time I've been holding this back—I wasn't sure that regular people would understand. I know it sounds retarded, but it has something to do with ghosts and/or aliens. And I'm not talking about the two guys who went looking for UFOs, discover a pickup truck FULL of Mexicans, and end up getting into a huge fight. I'm talking about REAL paranormal activity.

Plus, we might have some devastating evidence that (1) Hawaii isn't really a state and (2) ducks may have more uses than previously thought.

Yeah, totally. That's Mike Stevens. He saw the same shit I saw, and he's going to back up a lot of the stuff I'm saying.[2]

What's up.

Yo.

A lot of intellectuals are probably scoffing right now. That's fine. I totally respect that, and you can eat

---

[1] I'm sorry to interrupt, but Jeff Swibner, if you're reading this, you're a fucking fag. YOU KNOW WHAT I'M TALKING ABOUT. If you're not Jeff Swibner, please disregard.

[2] If one dude told you about something messed up, you'd be like OK whatever, and that would be the end of it. But if TWO DUDES told you about it, then even the most reasonable person would be like, Yo this is seriously messed up.

a dick, but trust me, even though me and Mike Stevens
don't work at any major scientific institutions or have
Nobel Prizes in our closets, we're a couple of earnest
motherfuckers. We saw something. And I'm so freaked out
about it that if somebody blew their nose really loud
right now, I'd burst into tears.

For those of you who aren't scoffing, *your mind must be
going nuts*. You've probably spent years trying to block
these ideas out of your head. Afraid that you might have
to reexamine some fundamental assumptions about the world,
maybe even have to carry around a stick or a knife or
something. But listen. That is exactly the unsuspecting
and carefree attitude of someone who hasn't seen a sock
slide across the kitchen floor because IT wanted to.

The very fact that you are reading these words means
that you got these feelings; I don't know, and that maybe
deep down YOU KNOW there is some weird shit out there.
I'm positive I'm not the only one who feels this way.
Maybe you never realized that you were searching for
something, but after thinking about ghosts and aliens for
even the last couple seconds, <u>you can sense it</u>. It might
have even happened before, when you heard some dude moan,
when there were no moaning dudes anywhere, and you sat
there, speechless. Or when you were at a stop light, and
you turned your head, and saw this owl just sittin' there
staring at you, and it *mouthed your name*. In that moment,
you knew that you were missing . . . something. You
reached for this book for a reason.

Look, I'm not saying that you have to reject the whole
conception of the universe. I'm just asking you not to
be a dick about ghosts and aliens. Scientists of Planet

Earth, don't you remember the first time you were like, *What the fuck?* Don't you want that feeling again?

Well, this is it. I've collected all my studies of the past week for you guys to check out. If you like it, cool, we can start making hypotheses and experimenting together. If not, well, don't be surprised when, out of nowhere, you're knocked on the floor, and see a mysterious wig sliding toward your face. At that moment, you'll wonder why you didn't believe us.

It's like the inventor Bill Telescope. Nobody believed him about his amazing invention until *it was too late*.

Yeah, totally. Or what about the guy who invented the potato chip. Did anybody know how big they were going to get? Everybody thought the idea was preposterous. EVERYBODY. And guess what . . . <u>they're everywhere now</u>.[3]

Look, if someone came to *my door* right now or called me up and said, "Dude, I just seen the weirdest thing ever," I'd be like, "Dude, I believe you." And the guy would be like, "For real?" And I'd be like, "Yeah."

So, dude, you got to believe us. If only one scientist reads this and realizes that there's some messed up stuff out there, then I did my duty. This may be the most scientific thing I have ever done in my life. My name is Trey Hamburger and I just want to tell the world about some weird shit.

Your future lab assistant,
Trey Hamburger
Leonard, Michigan, 2008

---

[3]See **Exhibit A:** The History of the Potato Chip at the back of the book for more information about the potato chip.

1.

FOOD OF THE RETARDS

LEGAL NOTE

i.)   You may not even understand some of the stuff I
      say. I'll be talking on these levels that most
      people may never ever be able to reach. (For those
      of you who smoke pot, you'll understand what I'm
      saying.)

ii.) Also, to any/all government or scientific officials
      reading this, the stuff presented here is me and
      Mike's. If you want to borrow any of it for an
      experiment or something, then you'll need to get
      our permission or the permission of our lawyers.

OK, here is the shit I've compiled so far.

SATURDAY

1:

The Incident

I don't remember anything obvious that happens during the day. I get really pissed and almost set fire to the house because my mom brings home chicken again. Good thing I don't. After that, things start going pretty good cause she tells me she's going on vacation in a week, and that's the closest thing to having her dead.

Later that night, my mom and I are watching a show about crunchy peanut butter and Derek Wood calls up. He starts telling me about how Jeff Trenton just started whaling on his neighbor over a stolen Cabo Chicken Sub Sandwich. I mean I know they're good, but I'm like, *Damn*. He then says he has to go take a piss for a second and he'll be right back. I look over at my mom and she's pretty shocked about all the work that goes into making one jar of peanut butter. Then I think I see her scratch her crotch, but I don't know for sure.

Your mom might have a yeast infection.

It's possible. Although her diet has been quite neutral, and she hasn't been eating much sugar. Anyway, listen to this. All of a sudden Derek comes back on the phone, and he's emotional as fuck. It's like his mouth is really dry, but he STILL keeps swallowing.

Apparently, he put some Hot Pockets *in the microwave* before he went to the bathroom. Then, when he got back, the microwave was empty and the Hot Pockets were already on the counter. He says he can't even chew them because of the fear inside. Hearing this, both of my elbows buckle, and, except for the usual stream of shaved vaginas, my mind goes completely blank.

I can't believe a thing like this could happen to someone I party with. First off, I'm a skeptic. I'm not somebody who's wild about ghosts; so I'm the last person to say it's a butler from Mars or something like that. But there is no fucking way that the plate of Hot Pockets could have slid out of a *closed microwave* and onto the counter from natural forces. Derek then tells me he has to go and I'm like "OK" and I finish watching that peanut butter show with my bitch mom.

OK, there is a *possibility* that Derek just forgot he took the Hot Pocket[4] out of the microwave, *something he's never done in his life*. But this is impossible for two reasons: (1) I've known Derek for over two years and that's something he wouldn't do. (2) This is totally something a ghost would do. (Trust me, if I were making this shit up, I'd be saying it was like ten Hot Pockets floating, not one. I'm not a dude who just says stuff.)

Nevertheless, the weirdest thing about it is that after Derek told me that story, nobody heard from him again until later that night.

#

---

[4]In case you're from the future and you found this book in an abandoned building, Hot Pockets are small microwaveable frozen meals that first started out in the U.S., but are now gaining huge momentum in Belgium and Turkey. The weirdest thing about the Pockets is that nobody knows who invented them. They just popped up, and people just started eating them.

KITCHEN
DIAGRAM:

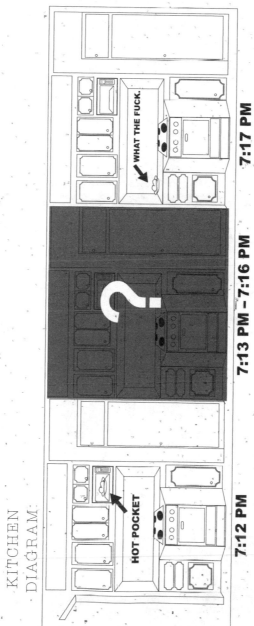

7:12 PM

7:13 PM – 7:16 PM

7:17 PM

HOW TO PREVENT/STOP A YEAST INFECTION
BY MIKE STEVENS[5]

All right ladies, LISTEN UP!
A yeast infection is when the vagina produces too much yeast, and continually itches. Are you willing to do WHAT IT TAKES to stop it from ever happening? Only _you_ have the answer to that question.

Now, if you're willing to avoid this kind of infection, you should pursue an aggressive yeast prevention plan. I know, it's pretty dorky, huh? But it serves a purpose—vagina maintenance.

1. Don't wear restrictive clothing that prevents your vagina from breathing.
2. Keep sugar and carbohydrate intake to a minimum, especially donuts.

So, is having a carefree attitude about your diet worth it? NO WAY!

Mike, how did you become such an expert in vaginas?

Ever since I saw my first vagina (in real life) I thought it was awesome, and it's become a matter of intense interest ever since. Plus I just want to help out the ladies when needed.

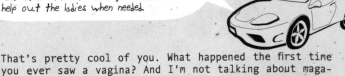

That's pretty cool of you. What happened the first time you ever saw a vagina? And I'm not talking about magazines, or babies, or your mom/aunt. I'm talking about a real live vagina of a nonrelative.

Well, a bunch of girls were viciously beating me with sticks outside my house. One of them was wearing a dress and her beaver was showing. I was like, "Wow." And that was it. I was hooked.

[5]The Oprah Winfrey Show, episode # 341, August 19, 2002, "Vaginas: Seriously—What's the Deal?"

2:

Two Pissed-Off Dudes

HOW is it that a man sees a Hot Pocket floating in midair, has his whole life rumpled up for a couple minutes, and nobody does a THING about it? Often, it is an event so intrinsically shattering that no man can defend himself. Some people may say, *Hey when you put stuff in perspective, that kind of thing won't bother you.* Well listen, the sudden tightening of your guts when somebody puts a knife to your throat is different than when a bird winks at you, <u>but it's still there</u>.

It's easy to laugh at people who say they've seen a Hot Pocket float. But what do we do when the laughter stops?

In some countries, like the Philippines, they talk about ghosts on the <u>front page of the news.</u> Do they know something we don't?

Any one of you could wake up tomorrow morning worrying about whether your neighbor is Indian or not, and by noon you can't even swallow because you start hearing these weird-ass footsteps that sound exactly like an old lady's—slow and tiny. This happens to millions of people all the time and there's pretty much no explanation whatsoever.

It's the same for me. One night I was having this dream, and in it I was looking at this piece of dream cardboard that had writing all over it. It was real foggy but I remembered the words exactly. Then I forced myself to wake up and write down the letters. It said "Eat a chicken burger" and later that day, I don't know how it happened, but I ended up eating one.

THAT'S THE KIND OF SHIT I'M TALKING ABOUT! People all across the globe are getting freaked out and everybody else is all "Yo, I gotta go help my grandpa out with some stuff, call me later." So these unexplained events will remain so until somebody, somebody who <u>doesn't give a fuck</u>, comes forward and speaks the truth about it. Well, that's all about to change right now.

At this point, you might be asking yourself why someone like me has suddenly acquired an intellectual curiosity after a lifelong passion for nonintellectual endeavors, like jerking my gherkin. Well, I think there are certain people who are chosen for weird-ass reasons to do some bad-ass shit. I'm probably one of those mysterious people. So now, fully aware of the sensitive, even dangerous ground I'm treading on, I am completely prepared to beat the shit out of a ghost if I have to. And, even though there's a lot of rich fucks out there who want me to keep quiet about this stuff, I believe doing so would be a crime against the scientific community, which I've been a member of now, for over a week.

Supposedly there's a hidden underground sanctuary in the Himalayas where the masters of world meet and talk about this sort of thing <u>all night long</u>.

Yeah, and there may even be a wave of deathbed confessions to come any day now too. But until that time, somebody needs to start talking about this stuff in an Open Forum, where people can express their frustrations and manage their emotions. Finally, for all you people out there who are sick of floating couch cushions or inexplicable squirting sounds, you don't have to be a victim anymore.

NOTE FOR SCIENTIFIC OFFICIALS:

In case there are any job positions in a scientific field, I'm definitely available. At my last job, my boss practically asked for my advice every day. He was a dipshit. I single-handedly saved the company from bankruptcy. Twice. The company was losing sales every day. (I wasn't supposed to know about that—so don't bring it up with my boss if you call him.) So I increased the sales and everybody backed me up. We had a party later that month about the sales and I talked to everyone there and they said it was because of me. So what can I say? You can give them a call, but I got to see if it's cool with them first. Then you can take the ball from there, I don't have a problem with **black**-skinned people either.

3:

Emotional Preparation

FACT: Everything you know is BULLCRAP.

FACT: There is shit going on that we can't even comprehend.

FACT: At any moment some dude could be watching you and you wouldn't even know it.

FACT: The government knows all this and won't say a word.

Before we go any further, you got to be ready for some major crap. Because I'm about to talk about some stuff that may very well mess up your entire life, and the lives of your buddies.

CLUES:

* Jeff Trenton beat Derek's neighbor's ass over a Cabo Chicken Sub Sandwich.

* A Hot Pocket teleported in Derek's kitchen.

When I was a kid, I remember I loved staying up late, looking at the stars, wondering about the _Mysteries of the Universe_ and then freaking out and screaming when I saw something move.

All right, I guarantee that this will make a frighteningly huge amount of sense and it might/will scare some of you. I apologize for that. If you're not intimidated yet, let me ask you this. Does the mere mention of severed heads scare the crap out of you? Or does the thought of some dude floating make you want to call a buddy and talk about it? If so, I'm going to tell you something: this isn't for you. Because the rest of this book is full of crap just like that, or worse. Most people simply can't handle it. Even though you think you could, I am pretty sure most of you would collapse on the floor in an instant. And for others, it will be hard to imagine that things like this actually do happen.

I used to live in a duplex that had to be blessed.

But these things do happen, every day.[6] Oh, and if you're one of those people who think that we should first be trying to the solve the world's socioeconomic problems, like child prostitution or the price of a taco, before we even THINK about dealing with ghosts/aliens, then try this: Imagine you're about to go to sleep at night and there's this really weird green face right outside your window, staring at you. Makes global politics seem meaningless, doesn't it?

Some idiots think that Transylvania is really just Pennsylvania.

---

[6]Mike went to college for like a week. He was only excited about going to one class, Anthropology, and that was because of Indiana Jones. But during the first day of class, the professor said that if anyone was in there because of Indiana Jones, they should get out. So he got out.

You might even be thinking, "Dude. I heard this story before, and I'm still alive." And yes, I KNOW, a pillow (acting alone) will never be able to do a hostile takeover of *Air Force One*, BUT what if there were several pillows acting in unison with each other? Puts things in a different perspective?

Now, for those of you who are ready to deal with an investigation this huge, I got to prepare you.

THE FEAR BARRIER

PARANORMAL ENTITY

ELECTROPHONIC SHIVER

MOTION RESPONSE

LIGHT RAYS

FUCKING RUN, DUDE

See a ghost → brain recognizes it and gets scared as fuck → sap is released into body → legs start running hard

Most people wouldn't even think about entering a super old house where one hundred years ago, some dude went nuts and got into a huge fight with his cats and birds and his other pets. This actually happened, and I won't bore you with the details, but the guy's nose was found two hundred miles away, stuffed with acorns. Most people would be thinking, "If I went there and I did see something, I would FLIP the FUCK OUT. I don't even know what I would do, but it wouldn't be cool, not at all."

If I saw a ghost, I would go at it.

Me too, no questions asked. But most people wouldn't. I think most people's instinct when they see a ghost or an alien would be to get out of there as fast as they can. But there are a chosen few who would instinctively fight it as well. So before we do anything we have to first deal with the fear barrier.

The most important thing you'll learn here: ghosts and aliens don't give a crap, and neither should you. And that's how you have to be when you're dealing with these guys. Tell yourself that you're crazy. That it doesn't even matter if you die because you saw some shit that only a couple people on Earth will ever see. You have got to break through that fear barrier because that's the only way.

If I wake up and hear something at night, I stab into the dark with my combat knife. And if that isn't sufficient, I bark furiously as I sweep the house with a baseball bat. Otherwise, I'm up ALL NIGHT.

SAFETY

The second thing we have to focus on is safety. You don't want to put yourself or any amigos in a position where they might unnecessarily get ionized. So here are some frequently asked questions about what to do when you're in the situation I'm in everyday.

What do I do if I hear some weird-ass noise?

Run.

What if a ghost starts fucking chasing after me?

Get to other people *fast*.

What if everybody's asleep?

Wake them up immediately. <u>This is your life</u>.

Does the same apply to aliens?

Yes.

What's the deal with these dead grandpas popping up and attacking people all the time?

I don't know. I'm sick of it, and that's what we're going to find out.

And what if I'm a regular dude—is there any way I could avoid this shit? This is NOT something I could handle.

Your best protection is the life you lead. If you're not cool at all, and basically a dick, then evil will cross your path. <u>But there is no guarantee.</u>[7]

In the end though, there's nothing that you can do to emotionally prepare yourself for a floating couch cushion or an alien going berserk in your backyard. So just keep a picture of Little Richard with you at all times, because it's impossible to stay scared when you look at it. And always have some peanuts handy in case you run into trouble and can't get to a food source. A single peanut can power your brain for over an hour. No joke.

A SIMPLE NOTE ON GHOSTS

Grief over losing a loved one is so powerful that if some dude asked you to hang out, you would most likely say yes, but you probably wouldn't be all festive and shit. So if somebody else's grandparent dies, then you can help out by crying with them and giving them emotional support. But remember, that grandpa is coming back, fucking shit up on Earth BIG TIME, and somebody is going to have to stop him. Don't believe me? Imagine that you're a dead grandpa. What would be the first thing you'd try to do?

I would first test out my new abilities, and help out my grandkids. Then I would try to kill as many living people as possible.

[7]Ed Trimmel got his nose bit by a goat, and Ed Trimmel is cool as fuck.

Exactly, Mike. Grandpas are cool when they're alive, BUT that doesn't mean that we should let our guard down when they're dead. We have to understand that a ghost's energy is deadlier than the deadliest poisonous gas in terms of the accuracy, intensity, and duration of its action—a fact that one of Bulgaria's senior-most diplomats agrees with.[8] (Note: If your grandpa was beheaded, then it's three times as likely he'll become a ghost. Expect action.)

Also, if you know somebody that's sick, don't let them go to a HOSPICE because, for some reason, everyone who goes in there comes out in a body bag.

[8]U.N. General Assembly Meeting Minutes, Resolution 69/164 of 22 November 1978, "Sacred Bleu!: Paranormal Combat Tips." Vladimir Gergoff, Bulgaria.

LEGAL NOTE:

The following letters contained within this scientific work *have all been sent to real live professors, scientists, and pastry companies.* Due to legal reasons, I cannot publish the exact name of ALL of those who have replied. Some have given me permission to publish their names, and some didn't. For those who didn't, they are basically dicks. So I made up a new name in place of theirs. For those who responded to me with the threat of possible legal action for using their letter even without their name—especially those whom I had explicitly called retarded—I have paraphrased their letter in the spirit of their response. (Oh, and by the way, Professor Timothyq Arnoldsq JERKS IT to *Cat Fancy* magazine.)

Trey Hamburger
681 Lake George Road
Leonard, MI 48367

March 8, 2008

Dr. Peter Bodenheimer
Astronomy & Astrophysics
201 Intordisciplinary Sciences Building (ISB)
Santa Cruz, CA 95064

Dear Dr. Bodenheimer,

For centuries, scientists thought there was only stuff
that exists. But recently, it has come to my attention
that there is some stuff that doesn't exist that really
does exist. Sounds like bullshit until you realize
Einstein said it. He didn't. But what if he did . . .
    During the last couple weeks, incidents in Berlin,
London, Moscow, Tokyo, and Leonard, Michigan, have pretty
much proved the existence of ghosts/aliens. And a lot of
people at the top are scared.
    For a long time I thought physicists were retarded,
because of what my mom said. And I'm sorry for that.
But now, my colleague Mike Stevens and I need to know
about the existence of ghosts and/or aliens. (A lot of
my associates are going nuts just thinking about the
possibilities: Jeff Trenton knows of several intergalactic
fights that have taken place—*dogfights*. So don't think
it's just us.)
    Now most scientists, I assume, say that aliens don't
exist because they're afraid people would go berserk and
run down the street and start swinging around katana
swords and not go to work the next morning because what's
the point. But look, me and Mike definitely wouldn't do
that. We won't start amassing a huge amount of knives and
armor for an intergalactic battle. Or go to some store
and just run out with an armful of cigarettes because
nobody will give a CRAP about prison after the invasion.
We'll chill, I promise.
    And don't worry, if you tell us, we won't tell anybody
it was you. We'll just say it was some dude we know, but
we'll never say exactly who.

Thanks a lot,
Trey Hamburger, a mature person who won't go nuts if he
finds out ghosts or aliens exist
Mike Stevens, another guy of similar nature

P.S. Please RSVP soon so me and Mike can start preparing
if we have to.

Do you think he'll fall for it?

If he believes we're a couple of emotionally mature people,
then maybe. Regardless, we'll have to wait.

Are you going to go nuts if
he says yes?

BIG-TIME. What about you?

Of course.

S U N D A Y

4:

The Investigation

THE morning after the teleporting Hot Pocket confrontation I call up Derek Wood and he's still wigged out about the incident, but is cool with me coming over to investigate.[9]

I roll up to the house. Supposedly, it was designed by Frank Lloyd Wright's cousin, Todd. It still sucks though. Derek runs out and meets me at my car. He's like, "Hey, I didn't want to tell you before, but my dad is like, retarded. So just to warn you . . ." I act like I'm cool with it, but I'm not. I can't believe he just dropped this bomb on me right before I'm about go in. And I know I can't turn back now because, well, whatever; I'm not getting into it, but I want to see a Hot Pocket float even if it means I might get clawed up.

When I go inside, the house is surprisingly well kept. But there is Disney shit EVERYWHERE. Disney placemats, wallpaper, cups. I guess I discover what Derek's dad likes.

I walk into the kitchen, where it all took place. I look back at Derek and he's still at the door. Won't even step into the kitchen. Even looks like he's going to throw up. He

---

[9]To avoid repetition, I won't be using the word "alleged" when I'm talking about something weird. It's more intense that way.

says he is so scared that he hasn't used the microwave at all, except for some cheese sticks that would've taken over an hour in the oven, which is justifiable I guess.

If you're dealing with ghosts/aliens there are no rules or absolutes. There are circumstances that facilitate ghost or alien contact, but there are no guarantees. So I wasn't expecting a Hot Pocket to start floating, BUT I was totally ready to punch one down if it did.

I sense a huge amount of negative energy vibrations near the kitchen counter. I approach softly. My mind probes the surrounding area, but there is a force field stopping me from going farther. I'm pissed.

Then I get this weird-ass feeling. My balls tingle, but I resist the urge to scratch them. I push my mind harder, and my pubes point right at the counter. My nipples enflame. The energy barrier is too strong.

I ask Derek for more info.

Derek Wood then starts telling me some of the most fucked-up shit ever. He's like, "Dude, I don't know if this is related, but I heard this story a couple weeks ago. This really old guy started telling me this when I was waiting in line at the grocery store. I forgot about it until the Hot Pocket Incident. He said

---

Do you think gay people would eat dick-shaped crackers?

Probably.[10]

---

[10]Please see **Exhibit B**: Proof that I Would Never Eat Dick-Shaped Crackers.

that one time back in the nineties near the old meatball factory, there was a bunch of hillbillies out in a field, just
hanging out. Then out of nowhere this UFO landed."
  I'm like, "What?"
  And Derek is like, "Yeah, I know. The really old guy said
that all the hillbillies were cool with it at first. Then the
door popped open, and the dudes watching started blinking
like crazy."
  I cautiously look over at Derek's microwave and I feel a
lot of energy in the area. Something is definitely here. I
also look around the room to make sure Derek's retarded dad
isn't there, waiting to leap out, either.
  "The really old guy said that everybody thought the aliens
would come out, take a few people, fuck 'em, and drop them
in the forest a couple hours later. But no. The aliens went
nuts. One alien came out, doing all these back flips, and
then started throwing rocks at EVERYBODY. One guy got hit
pretty bad, and everybody started running hard. Another dude
tripped, and this *other* alien busted out of the spaceship at
full speed and just started whaling on the guy with his flipper. Then the really old guy told me the flipper wasn't smooth
either. I asked him how he knew the flipper wasn't smooth,
and he lifted up part of his beard. And there, I could see a
couple little scratches that *couldn't have come from anything
made on Earth.*
  "Then the really old guy started talking about how Mr. Evans
ironed his shirt once while wearing it, and blew up his nipples.
It didn't have anything to do with the aliens, but it definitely
explained why no one has EVER seen the guy swimming."
  I tell Derek we have to get out of the kitchen. It's just
too weird in there. The energy.
  Thinking about his story, I get so mad about how careless
those aliens were. Somebody always gets hurt when rocks are
thrown. And I bet that really old guy was never able to get
a full-time job with that huge scratch on his cheek.

Who picks up the pieces when
something like THAT happens?

Right then I decide that I would probably dedicate my life
to stopping these beings on a full-time basis. It's pretty
hard to concentrate on daily activities when you know the
shit I know. Plus I can express a unique part of myself that
speaks the language of my soul—a part held back in the past
because I was afraid people would start saying shit.

Rebirth is always possible.

So this is the start of my huge-ass quest. I know this
mission may cost me a few amigos, but frankly I don't give a
crap. Sometimes one dude must live in darkness so other dudes
don't have to wig out. And, if I don't follow this through,
I may wake up one morning trapped in a cheese web, or *maybe
even something worse.*

For now, I don't know if any of those hillbillies are still
alive, but I have to talk to them. But I first need to see
that really old man's flipper scratch.

When I'm about to leave, it looks like Derek wants to say
something more about his dad, or retarded people in general.
But I pretend not to hear and start walking. But then, there
is this little pepperoni, like a Hot Pocket Pepperoni, on the
ground. I start running to my car, hard.

5:

A n a l y s i s

IT was just a regular pepperoni.
I ask Paul Hugs and his sister Pauline about it. That's all
they eat. It took them about one second for analysis.

*It's way too big to be
stuffed in a doughy microwavable bun along
with other similar ingredients.*

OK, WARNING, I think that somebody has caught on to the
investigation. Maybe it's just that I've become more aware and
sensitive to these things, but whatever is here in Leonard is
getting braver, and possibly dangerous. Today I notice that
the same dude is outside every morning when I drive to school.
It's fucked up. I drive past him this morning real slow to
check it out, and it's like he just stares right through me.
He is talking into his jacket too. (When I tell Jeff Trenton
about it Jeff says, *That son of a bitch.*)
I don't know if it's a hybrid, or perhaps even a pure-
blooded alien. When I have more information, I'll definitely
report on it.

Then at 18:30 EST, Mike Stevens and I encounter a sound so unsettling that it could possibly cause the whole pattern of one's life to disintegrate. Our imaginations cannot fathom the depths of evil that gave birth to such a noise.

It was a gurgle.

A really weird-ass gurgle.

As of yet, we are not sure if there is a connection between the Hot Pocket, the alien hybrid, and the gurgle. But we will report on it as soon as we know.

REPLY FROM GUY

> Dr. Peter Bodenheimer
> Astronomy & Astrophysics
> 201 Interdisciplinary Sciences Building (ISB)
> Santa Cruz, CA 95064

Mr. Hamburger,

I have received your letter regarding the existence of paranormal entities, and I have some thoughts that I would like to share with you. First, before I continue, please consider a few of the many fascinating concepts in science with which one could occupy oneself. For example,

- dark matter—does it exist? If so, will it ultimately cause the universe to pull back into itself?
- quantum superposition—how can the same particle be in two places at the same time?
- the beginnings of our universe—what are the mechanisms that brought about everything that exists?
- quantum entanglement—how can two particles affect each other instantly when they are light years away?

After considering these concepts as well as the many other fascinating ideas and puzzles in science, I do not understand why there is a letter on my desk asking whether one should prepare for an alien attack. I suspect it is because you have never been exposed to any formal science training. As for the existence of extraterrestrial entities, I can assuredly say there is little or no evidence. However, there is vast evidence for other strange and wonderful ideas *in science* and I encourage you to seek out those mysterious things and ponder them.

I hope this helps. If you have any other questions about this matter, please inquire elsewhere.

Cheers,
Peter

NATIONAL FEDERATION OF RETARDED PEOPLE
Okalahoma

NFRP
1234 Retard Road
Stupid Idiot, OK 47362924

Dr. Peter Bodenheimer
Astronomy & Astrophysics
201 Interdisciplinary Sciences Building (ISB)
Santa Cruz, CA 95064

Dear Dr. Bodenheimer,

Congratulations, YOU'RE IN.

Sorry,

Trey Hamburger, NOT the president

Trey Hamburger

Mike Stevens, also NOT the president

MIKE STEVENS

2.
OK, SERIOUSLY, WHAT'S GOING ON?

6:

History
of Leonard

THE prairies of Leonard were first owned by a
bunch of Navajos. Then, all of a sudden, some white people
busted out of the forest. The white people talked to the Navajos and, at first, the Navajos thought they were pretty cool.
So they both signed a treaty saying that the land would belong
to the Navajos forever. That treaty was broken fifteen minutes
later when gold was discovered. Then the white people named
the land after the guy who found the gold, Leonard.

Even though Leonard has suffered greatly from what's happened in the last couple days, this isn't the first time stuff
like this has happened. Below I have collected the accounts
from several local intelligence agencies, law enforcement
agencies, and dudes we know personally. We have scrutinized
these accounts, filtering out those that were even marginally
questionable, leaving us with the strongest case possible of
paranormal activity. Below are the following accounts.

1700s There was this Elizabethan guy. He had a horse and
rode it all the time. One day, out of nowhere, this giant
egg busted out of the forest and came right at him. The dude
just started puking all over his horse's mane. But get this,

SOME ELIZABETHAN GUY

the horse started puking too, from the sensation of having puke on its mane. They barely got away.[11]

1971 There was this guy and he was making a turkey, and it looked great, and everyone in the living room was like, "Where's the turkey?" And he was like, "It's coming." And then, out of nowhere, this mysterious face appeared in the window and the guy just started puking all over the turkey. Everybody went home. The host is in an insane asylum now.

1993 Todd "Semen" Niemen and his brother saw a vampire in their backyard and drove it away with gongs they found in the attic. And I ain't bullshitting. It happened, and it was fucked.[12]

Summer 1995 Somebody said that Josh Marshall caught a mermaid and kept it in his basement and had sex with it *whenever he wanted.* So far, there has been no conclusive evidence, except for him walking around all smug during that time period.

December 2, 1996 Jeff Trenton's dad woke up one morning, and his foot was gone.

August 17, 2002 Mike Stevens's uncle told Mike a macabre account of the time he thought he heard a bluegill say "pass the crackers" and ended up flipping his boat over on Walters Lake. The family warned him not to talk about his experience, fearing it would jeopardize his ultimately successful attempts at becoming a mystery shopper.[13] But now, with the job secured and the recent events, the information cannot be kept secret. (If Mike's uncle were making it up, he would have cast himself in more of a hero role.)

---

[11]*Horse News*, September 1784, Volume 8, No. 34, "The Egg's Back."
[12]Ask Todd "Semen" Niemen if you don't believe me.
[13]Mystery shoppers are people who go under cover as fake shoppers to make sure the workers aren't being dicks to the customers. I have worked at a place that gets mystery shoppers. So I know they're out there.

There's a certain intrigue to the life of a mystery shopper.

Summer 2003 Jeff Trenton shot a bottle rocket out of his ass.

2004 After the mysterious appearance of hundreds of sea cucumbers at several beaches near Walters Lake, Ed Trimmel grew a Mexican Mustache. Coincidence?

This is a true story, I swear. In 2004 Jessica Barnes accidently sat on a piece of uncooked chicken after getting out of the shower. Six weeks later she had eggs popping out of her beaver. The family smashed up all the eggs except one. They moved away when the neighbors started asking about the beaked baby.

2005 Todd Evans's cousin removed an alien implant from his nose. It was hard and yellow. He wiped it on the underside of a chair and pretty much forgot about it UNTIL NOW.

2005 This is 100 percent true. Jeff Trenton's dog just started looking at the corner of his living room and there wasn't anything there. Think about it. If you were a pet, what the hell would you stare at? Nothing, right?

What do you think actually goes through a dog's mind? CRAZY SHIT, THAT'S WHAT.

2006 Due to a sudden decrease in meatball consumption, the meatball factory in our town closes down. Nobody understands why.

Two Days Ago The Hot Pocket thing happened with Derek.

Today Some new guy moves in and acts really weird. It may be nothing, but I noticed the previous neighbor who lived in the *same house* was working in his garden a few weeks before 9/11. Certainly not a coincidence.

Now, the thing about ghosts/aliens targeting small places like Leonard is that a lot of things like NORAD are in these smaller places. And that's where all the main guys are going to be when shit goes down. Not the biggest cities, where they know they're dead with the first attack. But if you go somewhere not worth blowing up . . . then there you go. This is the mentality of a ghost/alien.

It's clear that there's a lot of people at the top who know what's going on. (Look at _Exhibit C_: A Seemingly Innocuous Document from One Colonel to Another in the back for more information.) There are even some in government that say we got seven years tops, and it's time to party up.

And since Saturday there have been more than a hundred other circumstantial reports, mostly of the squirting sort. As for now, all we can do is speculate. So me and Mike just sit there, and speculate.

MINOR CLARIFICATION

Since we're digging up the past, I have to clarify an event that occurred earlier this morning. OK, Jake Harker, if you're reading this, listen up. Remember that time when you left my house and came back five minutes later *without warning* and saw me sitting on the couch with my pants down? OK, now listen. I wasn't jerking off.

Trey wouldn't do that. He's cool.

I was merely airing out the skin in my pelvic region. It was getting itchy and I wanted to get some sun on that area. You might not be familiar with anaerobes, but they're tiny bacteria that can create smells and slight irritation when unattended. Sunlight and air is a common method for killing anaerobes. SO LET IT GO.

Thanks, Mike. It's a shame I even have to explain myself in this instance. People should know I wouldn't do that.

7:

Following the Clues

OK, that demon hybrid I thought was following me is just a regular guy who moved in down the street, but nobody thought it necessary to fucking alert me. BUT from the shit my sources have been telling me, the mismatched clothing, and the faggoty flute sounds, there's a chance he's from another dimension, or India. There are even some people who live around there, and I personally know the people, who have heard screams coming out of that place. If there is any sacrificing going on in there, then that's bullshit.

I'll keep you updated for sure.

CLUES:

* Aliens throw rocks at hillbillies.

* Really old guy gets smacked with an extraterrestrial flipper, hard.

I used to live near a couple of Asian guys who loved to wrestle.

I still totally think someone is following me though. This morning an unidentified voice called me up on the phone and told me to give up my investigation. By the time I told them to eat a dick, *they were already gone.*

My main goal now is to see that hillbilly's flipper scratch. Intellectually, this is the best route. So I have to find the really old guy. At this point, I'm totally willing to talk to poor people even if it means I'll be putting myself way out of my comfort zone, or even in the position of getting raped.

Where do hillbillies hang out? My first experience with them was a couple years ago. On Valentine's Day, this hillbilly girl in class got a handmade book from her hillbilly boyfriend. No chocolates or flowers or anything. The little book contained "love coupons" for hugs, kisses, backrubs, and there was even a coupon for her boyfriend to be her slave for the day. Basically, a bunch of free shit. And I thought, so that's what poor people do for Valentine's Day.

Ever since that class, I haven't seen any hillbillies. So I have no idea where to look.

I ask my aunt, who's an idiot, if she knows. She says "No" in a real bitchy voice. She thinks she's British, but she's not.

I talk to my neighbor on the left side, and he's dumb so he doesn't know either. He goes to one of those churches where the really wild stuff happens.

So Mike and I go home.

Then, out of nowhere, Jeff Trenton busts into my basement and runs toward me and Mike Stevens. *His face is utterly bloodless.*

Mike immediately gives Jeff a glass of pop. Then Jeff is like, "Dude, Derek's dead."

8:

Dead Amigos

APPARENTLY, Jeff Trenton heard it from Todd "Semen" Niemen and Todd heard it from his cousin. As Jeff tells us the whole story, Mike and I slowly chew our burritos.

And Jeff is like, "All right, it's dark as fuck. And there isn't anybody around. Derek Wood is just lying on the couch watching TV. So far no big deal. But then, all of a sudden, this whistling sound starts going off BIG TIME. Derek sits up like an electric hair, and throws the blanket on the floor _hard_. His heart is going nuts with fear. Then these milk spots start forming all over his shirt for no reason at all. He starts yelling, even _harder_."

Jeff swallows, then continues.

"Now listen to this. Derek's dad comes home two hours later, and BOOM drops a huge bowl of potato salad on the floor because of the horror. He runs to the living room, and Derek _is nowhere_. All he sees is a little gut on the carpet. Then some sad-ass music starts playing and Derek's dad just starts puking up all this potato salad all over the couch. Puke drips off the cushions _real slow_.

"Then Derek's dad looks out the window and just starts wondering, but he doesn't see shit because it's dark as fuck."

Jeff Trenton falls into the couch and can't speak anymore.
I imagine Derek Wood floating around in the netherworld,
or some other dimension, not knowing what the hell is going
on. A strange bubble passes by Derek's face, and he punches
at it.

Now Jeff Trenton is the kind of guy that if you give him
a few wine coolers, he starts saying the weirdest stuff ever
(secret bubble baths with his grandpa and stuff like that),
but this seems different. Usually if some dude were to say
that shit to me, I would be like, *Big whoop*. But he says it
like he meant it. So I'm like, *Shit.*

*If these were just mere
fantasies, they would not follow such a
chillingly logical course.*

Then, out of nowhere, Jeff Trenton sits up, moves in closer,
and speaks in a lowered voice. He asks us if we have any burritos left. We say no. He then just starts running out of the
house. We just sit there, quietly chewing our burritos and
silently freaking out.

Treyq Hamburgerq
681 Lake George Road
Leonard, MI 48367

March 9, 2008

Professor David Epstein
Assistant Professor of Biophysics
Nebraska Center for Biology and Chemical Science
Mount Clemens University
Lincoln, NE 68588

Dear Professor Epstein,

My name is Treyq Hamburgerq. This is not my real name. I
would be stupid and suicidal to reveal that information.
For reasons you will understand later I cannot divulge my
identity. I will also be careful as to what I reveal to
you, because any of it could be cross-referenced against
a list of people who are privy to the knowledge I have.
So I have made sure I am totally untraceable. (The above
address is NOT my mom's house.)

People like me and my vaporized ex-colleague have
been exposed to information so highly classified that
even the *President of the United States of America* is not
automatically entitled to view it. As you can imagine,
having such powers means that I also have access to a
lot of delicate and sensitive information, as did my
colleague, which ultimately led to his evaporation.

Here's what's going on.

I'm sitting in my kitchen right now with the lights
out. There's a mysterious gurgling noise coming from a
couple houses down—the "Indian." On Saturday, the same
being said that his speech was slowing down and mentioned
something about *energy running low*. A human may say
something like that, *but it's rare*. We also found droppings
behind Mikeq Stevensq's house which, after analysis, look
like pumpkin pie. I have extra stool samples if you're
interested. (<u>Can you receive packages at the address
above</u>?) Some people are even saying that the guy ionized
Derekq Woodq, but nobody knows for sure. Any advice would
be gravely appreciated. And if you don't get another
letter from me, I'm probably stuck in a transdimensional
cheese web.

Stay safe,
Treyq Hamburgerq

P.S. Tell the world about me if the cheese thing happens.
And if your new role affects your personal life, I
apologize ahead of time.

REPLY FROM GUY

March 19, 2008

Trey Hamburger
681 Lake George Road
Leonard, MI 48367

Mr. Hamburger,

I cannot help you with this matter. Please do not mail
anything to my address.

Thank you,
David Epstein

   The biggest thing of the century is happening and nobody
wants to help us out!

MONDAY

9:

Possible Suspects

OUR meal is a gloomy one, and except for the quick conversation regarding whether or not Dawn Baynard is going to have sex with Eric Koller—

CLUES :

* Some guy is following me. He could be from another dimension, or India

* Derek Wood is dead, or at least stuck in space/time.

* A gurgling noise has been heard throughout the town, starting yesterday.

Dawn fed him a pretzel yesterday.

—our conversation is in complete silence.

The curious sound that we liken to a gurgle now fills the stillness of our minds. In the last couple days, we encounter this eerie gurgling, permeating our days with a continuous gurgling sound, like a tomato stuck in some guy's throat. Sometimes it would be coming from Mike's backyard. Other times, we would hear it hovering above us from outer space. And every so often it feels like it's coming from our deepest catacombs.

The vagueness of its origin distresses us more than if we were to see the actual dude doing it. In all my years of hanging out, eating tacos, and chasing Mexicans, I have never heard any sound like this. We'd be playing basketball, and then, during a free throw, we'd hear the gurgle. The next moment we'd all be running. This gurgle, wherever it's coming from, is RULING OUR DAMN LIVES.

All of this points to one thing: The "Indian."

Nobody has seen the "Indian" guy for over two days now. Todd "Semen" Niemen was supposed to be watching his house, but Todd's grandpa got a new computer and had to go on the ham radio webpage right away. So Todd's been over there neglecting his surveillance duties. Now, the "Indian"/alien hybrid could be out scurrying around all over town.

Some say the "Indians" are guarding something BIG.

I believe it. I phone Jeff Trenton, and he runs over. I tell him that nobody was watching the "Indian" when Derek evaporated, and he is like, *damn.*

This isn't the first "Indian" who came to Leonard either. Everybody thought the other one was harmless. He would always be slam dancing, and showing people his bumblebee tattoo. Sounds pretty cool, huh? Well think again, suckers. Deepak went back to India and strangled a goat.[14]

Yeah, I was surprised when I heard that.

[14]Taken from Josh Marshall's personal testimony at Ed Trimmel's house. August 18, 2005, 3:12 a.m. E.S.T.

I wasn't.

That's the thing. Nobody believed me at the time. And now, we got a similar situation with the Hot Pockets and the aliens and this new "Indian"/interdimensional entity and STILL NOBODY BELIEVES ME, except Mike and Jeff.

Derek did too.

I can't even think about that right now.

Now, we need to focus. The last time anyone saw the hybrid, he was roaming around the botanical gardens, grubbing for roots—which doesn't fit any known pattern of Indian behavior yet.

What's a botanical garden?

It's just a shitload of plants. He was probably collecting samples for his superiors. Todd also found out that he doesn't have a favorite song. That's another clue he's not from Earth, if we weren't already sure. In any case, I'm fairly confident in my assessment of *conventional* Indian mentalities.

He drank a glass of pop by lapping it up.

SON OF A BITCH!

OK, this is not a problem that can be resolved from writing our elected leaders or by making public statements. It is a monumental crisis that can only be amended by the use of crossbows and martial arts. If something is going to happen, it will happen on our terms, with us swinging around nunchakus.

Now we prepare for our first mission. Plus we need very definitive answers to the legal questions we would encounter.

It is vital for us to define what constitutes a legal right to attack an "Indian," or a pastry.

BROADSWORD TECHNIQUES

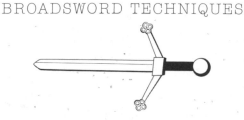

The Legendary Broadsword

LEGAL NOTE
   At the outset of this discussion, it is important for me to emphasize that the opinions expressed about broadsword techniques are my own and the CIA/DELTA FORCE neither endorses nor condemns any of the claims contained herein.

Living in the suburbs we've seen a lot. We're basically pit fighters.

I've seen a fully grown man taken down by a fucking chipmunk.

Evan Worton almost strangled Brett Sogal with a pair of sweatpants LAST WEEK. And Scott Hank went to punch Andy Pats, but ended up hitting Andy's belt buckle instead and went down hard. All this we have witnessed firsthand. We did not seek to become experts in the fighting arts, it was bestowed upon us, and we cannot withhold this knowledge in times like these.
   Now listen carefully. I have written this for people who

want to know what ghost/alien self-defense *is*, not what it *ought to be*. I have to warn you to take these techniques seriously. To give you an idea of how complicated and demanding these moves are, let me debrief you. This dude Kevin we know busted up Todd "Semen" Niemen's mom's birdhouse when he jumped off the roof. So we can't practice over there anymore. That was just the first half hour, not even on a real mission. It's a statistic that emphasizes the dangerous nature of our training. So make of that what you will.

In this section, I will talk about the broadsword, which I'm personally against, but in light of current events, its flagrant use seems reasonable. It is also one of the most powerful weapons that anyone with a colorful past can purchase legally.

Athough, if you have serious, unaddressed emotional issues, you should see a counselor before you begin your broadsword training.

Below I have included some broadsword techniques should you ever need them. Although this doesn't give you complete readiness for combat, the emphasis on weapons training up-front is a strategic necessity. The purpose of this program is to bring you to basic competency with the broadsword. You are learning techniques that could save your life or the lives of your amigos. Some of these moves are so risky that nobody relishes using these methods, no matter how cool they look.

EXTREME CIRCUMSTANCES ONLY

However, if you embrace evil thoughts during practice, your training will backfire.

The Broadsword Thrust is the quickest method in disabling your opponent. You could be like, *Excuse me, did you know that a single egg could*—BOOM, you got him. It's the kind of move you can only do once because if you try that egg question again, they'll probably hold up a shield.

I think the nations of the world should teach their peoples stuff like this.

We can't expect anything less.

OK, after your opponent knows you want to kill him for sure, there is no need to act like you're cool with him. You can now pursue more exaggerated moves like the Downward and Sideways Strikes, which basically consist of you whipping around the broadsword NONSTOP.

However, after training with the broadsword for some time, you'll become more aware of the realities of war.

Plus, merely knowing you could chop off some dude's leg will give you a feeling of wholeness, peace, and well-being.

I CAN KILL ANYONE I WANT.

It is true—a certain quietness creeps into the lives of those who practice the broadsword.

Gregory Kelto
City Council Member
PO Box 820
Leonard, MI 48367-0789

Treyq Hamburgerq
681 Lake George Road
Leonard, MI 48367

Mr. Treyq Hamburgerq,

Thank you for your inquiries. We have received your third letter requesting information about the specifics of self-defense law.

The ability to defend oneself from physical harm is a right recognized by Article 1, Section 6 of the Michigan Constitution. Although *you may be culpable for any injuries that you may inflict on an individual if you are NOT acting in self-defense.*

So far as I know there is no "The Federal Combat Act [that] explicitly forbid[s] one dude from attacking another if the dude didn't do anything obvious." While I am glad that you fully respect the philosophy behind that Act if it were to exist, neither the mayor—nor any individual—has the power to suspend similar laws if "the dude was seen doing something messed up."

However, if you have a dispute with an individual, and you are *not in immediate bodily harm,* you are not legally permitted to "attack."

Further questions about the law of Addison Township or inquiries about requesting a restraining order can be directed toward the Oakland County Sheriff's Department, Addison Township.

Your letters have been filed in case of any future incident.

Thank you,

Gregory Kelto
City Council Member

c.c. Chris Kimbel, Oakland County Sheriff

10:

The Mission

MANY of us are waiting for the second shoe to drop. Mike and I are done waiting, and are going to take aggressive action. The saddest thing is that after the second shoe actually DOES drop, many will still be waiting for the third shoe.

Just because something is against the law, doesn't mean that it's illegal. A hundred years ago it was illegal to wear a fake mustache to church, or become the governor of Michigan if you participated in a duel.[15] Now, those laws have been overturned *because they were wrong*. Although the city council has authority over this territory, Mike and I decide that this is way bigger than them, the law, or even us. So we plan to get inside that "Indian" house and figure out what's going on before he slimes another amigo.

Our mission will not be easy. If it were, we would not be here now, for other men would have already finished the task we now so nobly face.

The "Indian" base is approximately 220 meters from my house. We decide to wait till night to execute our reconnaissance mission, and perhaps make contact. Jeff Trenton comes over

[15]Internet.

with his crossbow, and Mike debriefs him. Jeff says he's
willing to kill, if we can give him any information about the
being's physiology, social structure, command structure, and
EXACT telepathic abilities. (Jeff collects swords.)

*I remember reading that they
are wary of ducks.*

Jeff nods his head real slow, and loads the crossbow. Mike
thinks he saw some drool drip from Jeff's mouth onto his
shirt.

JEFF TRENTON: A LIFE

What motivates a man? It's a complex question. Perhaps
no one will see into Jeff Trenton's heart and find the
true reason for his bloodlust. Or understand what exactly
happened the day he whaled on his neighbor about the Cabo
Chicken Sub Sandwich.

Textbook anal sadist.

Plus, he's still wanted in Macomb County for trying to cash a 34 million dollar check at a Citibank
drive-through. And for this, we have purposely chosen to
keep Jeff ignorant of certain sensitive information. We
understand that he's useful, but his erratic behavior is
liable to compromise some of the more delicate aspects
of the mission. Deceiving your buddies is dangerous, but
sometimes it's necessary.

Plus, there's no way we're letting him be a Central Commander after he shot a bottle rocket out of his ass that summer.

So for now, we'll leave it at that.

Me and Mike leave Mike's basement at 11:01 p.m. EST to begin the "Indian" Surveillance Mission. First, we check the sky. Empty. So we start out walking. No problem. Initially we get freaked out thinking about what could happen. I mean, the "Indian" could throw a bag of cobras or scorpions at us. Or we might open the door, and who knows, it could be on the floor squiggling around, covered with all these bone trinkets and amulets.

I look back toward Mike Stevens's house, and think about all the times we threw a Frisbee in his backyard, and how we should probably be doing that instead of risking our lives. But then in my vision, I see the "Indian" jump out the bushes and tackle Mike as he catches the Frisbee, and it starts clawing at his face. This must be done.

So we continue walking.

It is dark, but not too dark. For some reason, all the dogs lose the will to bark, and all the cats lose the will to meow. Earlier, the newscasters on TV said that something messed up was going to happen, but they didn't know what. Fog is everywhere. As we approach the house, some real smooth techno music starts pumping in our hearts. And me and Mike look at each other, and I'm like, "Are you ready for this, Kemo Sabe?" And he's like, "Yeah."

Dude, it was a night just like this. And there was this guy. And, from what I remember, I guess he was in his bedroom for two days watching movies, eating cabbage, and violently farting. Problem was, he had all the doors and windows tightly shut. The guy was found a week later ...dead.

Mike Stevens's story emphasizes the fragility of our lives.
We draw our steak knives and are ready to kill anything that
comes near us. We approach the house, and there's a light on
upstairs.

Before we go any closer, we reaffirm our commitment to beating the entity's ass and backing each other up, no matter
what. But then, out of nowhere, a moan comes out from the
upstairs window, "This bathwater is *perfect.*"

Jeff Trenton immediately goes home.

This whole thing is beginning to look like a lot more than a
routine "Indian" Surveillance Mission. We check the back door
and it's open. Mike and I slip through, totally noiseless. It
leads to the basement. As we walk in, I am ready for an attack.
But at first, there is nothing. Then I look down. *The floor is
peppered with pepper.* A sickening certainty washes over us—of
what we don't know. Inside, there are boxes everywhere. We
look in one. Bird magazines. It likes birds. And on the wall,
there is a watercolor painting of some fat lady.

When I look at a painting, there's nothing in my head except a buzzing sound.

After Derek Wood evaporated, everybody said that the
"Indian"/hybrid did it. But nobody really knows for sure,
except Derek's retarded dad. And he never said another word,
although if he did, it would sound like a bird chirping, and
we couldn't understand him anyway. Now we are about to find
out the truth, if we don't die in the process.

We walk up the stairs toward the light, and all we hear is
the sound of water droplets.

And there it is, in the tub.

His grooming is flawless. THIS ISN'T A DRILL. We hold our
positions, and so does it. The being looks up at me and says,
"Well, what do you want?" My butt puckers with fear. Mike
throws a bag of hers on him, and we start running hard. I
start choking because I'm running with potato chips in my

mouth. As we jump down the stairs, we hear it kicking around
and splashing like crazy.

The "Indian" sizzles profusely.

If rumors are true about hybrid aliens absorbing nutrients
through their skin, then *we got him.* We run out to Walters
Lake, the rendezvous point. *Jeff* Trenton is hopefully somewhere safe.

After we get to the lake and think about what we did, we
feel like idiots a little bit. We totally didn't have enough
weapons, and that thing could have shot spores at us. Fortunately, the "Indian" appeared to be in diplomatic mode, so
its combat symbiotes were not fully extruded. Next time we
may not be so fortunate . . .

Never before had we been in such direct conflict with enemy
powers. Had we reacted with any less courage, he would have
slain us. We stared into the face of death and survived. Our
daring mission, *although not mistake-free*, was successful
enough to restore some luster to the reputation of humans
everywhere. Will the people of the future understand the turmoil we went through and the losses we took?

One should hope they never will.

With the wind blowing all over our faces, we look over the
lake and reflect, hard.

11:

T u e s d a y

NOTHING weird happens in the morning. Josh Marshall leaves a few messages on my phone that the "Indian" hasn't made a move yet this morning. It knows we know. So things will be different now. Right now my nervous system is pretty calm, but who knows what could happen.

In biblical terms, this is a Holy War.

CLUES:

* The "Indian" likes bird magazines.

* The being is susceptible to herbs—induces sizzling.

Now, we have to prepare for a counterattack.

> I once attempted to fight those aliens without weapons, sleep paralysis and all. _One of the stupidest things I've ever done._

Dude, you never told me about this. What happened?

> One time, when I was sleeping, I felt a shadow caressing my hair. I immediately went into **combat mode**. The problem was I couldn't move. The creature knew this, and laid a log exactly where my own butt had been _seconds before_. Man, I want to KILL just thinking about it.

Going into combat mode[16] was probably your only option, but dude, you got to let that go after some point. It's over and you got to move on.

> That shadow almost ruined my damn life.

---

[16]For those unfamiliar with the fighting arts, **combat mode** is when your whole body tightens up and your jaws and fists clench shut. From there, your mind goes blank, and you strike at any movement, sometimes killing. This lasts for a couple seconds, and must be used only under extreme circumstances.

Trey Hamburger
681 Lake George Road
Leonard, MI 48367

March 10, 2008

National Neck and Spine Research Association
South Plaza Tower
5th Floor
Lexington, Kentucky 40506

Dear NNSRA,

Below I have included my research grant proposal titled
Ghosts/Aliens. Please let us know if we get the grant.

PRELIMINARY RESEARCH PROPOSAL FORM

Name of principal applicant: Trey Hamburger, Mike Stevens
Institution: Mike's Basement (Temporary)
Address: 706 Lake George Road
   Leonard, MI 48367

Title of proposal: Ghosts/Aliens
Duration: Couple weeks
Amount: $100,000,000; or if that's not
   possible, 40 bucks

HOW DOES YOUR WORK DESCRIBED FALL WITHIN THE ASSOCIATION'S RESEARCH STRATEGY?

All right, you're like the fifth person we talked to. So
far nobody seems to want to help out and we're sick of
it. So, I'm going to break it down quick. Mike Stevens
and I are forming an Elite Fighting Force. And we want
you guys to be a part of it.

WHAT IS THE POTENTIAL FOR CLINICAL/PUBLIC HEALTH BENEFIT ARISING FROM THIS STUDY?

First off, let me give you some backstory.
   Two days ago, I was in my room on my computer, and
out of nowhere I start smelling this fish smell. (I
remembered hearing that the smell means there is a
poltergeist nearby in the area. I got this from the
History Channel.) And this isn't the first time weird
shit has happened right after that smell. So I'm pretty
freaked at this point because I'm like, Shit, what's going

to happen this time? So I stand up real slow and start to walk out of the room because I don't want to be there when shit starts to go down. But then, out of nowhere, I hear this loud gurgling sound. So I'm like, HOLY SHIT, and I just start flying down the stairs and run out of my house, and chill at Todd "Semen" Niemen's basement for the rest of the day.

OK, explain that.

Other people shouldn't have to go through what I have. My proposal is to stop such things from ever happening again.

We have a six-tier plan to tackle this problem. However, I cannot show you it until you show us some money first. I've been warned of institutions that ask to see people's ideas and then turn around and start doing it themselves and act all innocent. (Did you know that the scarf was NOT invented by Mitch Jones, but really by his neighbor, Klaus von Diefendorf, the hunchback? Few do.)

In conclusion, I know there is some dumb shit people want to research and there just isn't enough money for everyone. So even if you people say no at first, that's cool. We'll still let you guys join up in case you change your mind. (I know people can change their minds. My friend Dawn Baynard said that she would definitely NEVER sleep with a man right away, or, anyway, that's what she thought until she met Bingo.)

Thank you,
Trey Hamburger

P.S. You ever wonder why you never see bald pigeons? . . .

FULL SPECIFICATIONS REGARDING GHOSTS/ALIENS:

THEIR WEAKNESSES AND HOW TO FIGHT THEM

The first American to orbit the globe saw some UFOs up there. When he got back into the ship he told the whole crew about it. Everybody went wild talking about the possibilities and nobody slept the whole ride home. When they finally returned, a newslady asked them about the UFOs, and all the astronauts said it was pretty awesome and couldn't wait to go back.

That's one way of looking at this whole thing.

Space is supposed to be empty.

That's another.

Mike and I subscribe to the latter interpretation. And that's why we have begun our full-scale assault.

Here we will expose their tactics, why they do what they do, and who they are. We have developed a short fact sheet about ghosts/aliens, much of it obtained from intercepted transmissions.

My phone's having some quirk, and it's interfering with other people's phones. From this, we have discovered things that cannot be explained. Plus I can hear my neighbor talk, and she never shuts up about her damn baby.

Every species, every living creature, has a weakness, so there is always going to be a way to beat your opponent. <u>No one is unbeatable</u>.

Take, for example, the dolphin. At first glance, dolphins seem invincible. They live in impenetrable caverns under the sea. They have sonar tracking abilities and spear-like noses. However, the problem is that while these creatures are smarter than the average person, they could never compare to the smartest humans. Dolphins could not advance technologically because they don't have hands and they live in water, making it basically impossible to forge metals for swords and shields. So it's like dolphins are forever stuck in the Stone Age! So their basic weakness is that we could just put them into a pool and then shoot machine guns at them.

Dolphins are smart, but not that smart.

Exactly. I used dolphins as an example here, but the same goes for ghosts/aliens/"Indians." We have to use the same reasoning.

THE ENEMY: WEAKNESSES

- These beings have a similar biological makeup and vulnerability to ballistic trauma. I'm sure a well-placed kick to a weight-supporting joint would instantly bring them down.

Think of it this way. No matter how strong a skull is—if enough force is applied, <u>it will pop</u>.

- They're egg bearers—*and those eggs can be smashed.*
- Most don't even like looking at each other if it isn't breeding season. This means they can be played against each other, politically <u>and emotionally</u>.
- The pressure points on an alien are exactly opposite from those of a salamander.

- If you can get close enough to glue a magnet on their head, their homing abilities will be useless.
- They probably have suction-cupping abilities to grip food since there is no gravity resistance in outer space—THOSE CUPS CAN BE CLOGGED.

This whole thing is starting to remind me of my first encounter with a Mexican. (Almost died.) That's a whole other story, though.

HOW TO FIGHT THEM

Even if our knowledge doesn't match up to theirs, there are still ways to fight them. Ghosts/aliens attack under the cloak of darkness. These guys will first send a paralysis beam through your window. If that beam touches your head, you will immediately pass out.[17] Our own government has microwave devices that can make people sneeze at vast distances—so this type of technology isn't absurd. You need to avoid this beam if you want to even begin thinking about close combat.

Since they usually attack during your sleep cycle, it's necessary to practice waking up without moving. That way, they'll think you're asleep and that it's cool to come in close, and then you can muster an enormous strength and lash out.

LASH OUT BILLY, LASH OUT.

Personally, if I ever get hit by the beam and they drag me into the ship, I'll really mess shit up in there BIG-TIME. I'll pop one of the side panels open and chew up all the circuitry and then swing my arms around, knocking down all the navigation systems. Wires will be hanging out and sparks will be flying everywhere. And one alien will look at another and be like, "We just picked up the wrong dude. That guy is awesome." Then the spaceship will explode.

---

[17]For more information about alien abduction see **Exhibit D:** *The Alien Abduction Test*

Served.

Many people might think I'd be too sedated to do this, but Mike put twenty-five blankets over me in a Simulated Abduction Scenario and I busted free like it was nothing.

However, in the rare situation you have time to prepare for an attack, make sure you have some type of spear or melee weapon. If you can see them, GO FOR THE HEAD. If you can pop it, their whole body will shut down. But you must remember that each hemisphere of an alien's brain is separated by a thick wall of bone. So if you're going to puncture the head, you have to hit both hemispheres *at the same time.* If you don't destroy both hemispheres, the other remaining one will be used as a spare and send out telepathic messages for back up.

Solid Bone

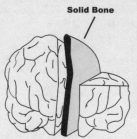

ALIEN BRAIN CROSS-SECTION

The biggest problem regarding aliens, or any transdimensional beings for that matter, is that they can telepathically deduce what you're going to do. Any premeditated attack will likely result in disaster—if you've got a crossbow under your blankets, an alien will already know this and thus will have the appropriate armor and shielding ready.

One way to counteract this is to think about something other than broadswords or spears right before you swing a broadsword or spear. How confusing would it be if some dude is thinking about wicker furniture while beating another dude's ass?

Very.

If you do stuff that doesn't make sense, an alien will quickly abort an abduction because it can't respond appropriately and doesn't want to deal with your bullshit at the moment.

Many times, an alien would rather leave than respond to some guy running around with his pants around his ankles.

If all else fails, simply act all submissive and wimpy, and then when they get close, start punching like crazy.

P S Y C H I C   T H O U G H T

Since the Hot Pocket Incident and our newly found consciousness of the Unknown, Mike and I are having premonitions, or psychic thoughts. Like, right now . . .

I'm hesitant to say this, because even as I write it, I realize how odd it feels/sounds. All right, I'm getting a premonition that there will be some dude, it's going to be in the Midwest, the states Ohio or Nebraska are shown in my head, who is going to get his ass beat bad. I predict that there will be some dude out there who will be reading this and he'll be like, "Is he talking about me?" and, a few months later, that very dude will walk outside his front door, and a couple of guys, who he **thought** *were cool, will just start whaling on him.*

Dear dude who's about to get his ass beat bad, <u>you need to listen carefully</u>. On August 14, three days before the incident, you will feel inclined to comment on a certain person's haircut. **DON'T.**

Seriously, dude. It's not worth it.

REPLY FROM LADY

National Neck and Spine Research Association
South Plaza Tower
5th Floor
Lexington, KY 40506

March 20, 2008

Trey Hamburger
681 Lake George Road
Leonard, MI 48367

Dear Trey Hamburger,

We have received your preliminary research proposal form
requesting grant monies from the National Neck and Spine
Research Association. Thank you for taking the time to
apply.
   It is our priority to choose the top candidates for
grant monies to assist in clinical trials that will
further research of the neck and spine. After careful
consideration, we have decided to pursue other applicants
for this grant at this time since your grant proposal
includes nothing about the neck or spine. Please note
that your application will be kept on file for six months
if a need arises for us to contact you in the future.
   I hope that this survey of the reviewers' comments,
which obviously center on the need for a scientifically
acceptable research design, will prove informative. If
you are interested in the guidelines that the National
Neck and Spine Research Association currently favors with
regards to proper controls in clinical trials, please
feel free to contact our institution again.

    Please accept our best wishes in your future endeavors,
and we thank you for your interest in the National Neck
and Spine Research Association.

    Cordially,

    Jesse Ordonez
    Grant Research Committee

Man, I thought they would be more sympathetic to this sort of thing.

What the fuck? Why is it so tough?

Dude, think about the Abe Lincoln impersonator. I'm sure there's a point in his life where he says, "That's it. I've reached a ceiling and I can't go any further with this." But then, <u>there's a breakthrough</u> and it makes it all worth it.

You're right. We got to keep going.

12:

Beard Detection

UNTIL Mike and I receive funding for laser cannons and supercomputers, we use whatever we have to defend
ourselves. For the last couple days, I've been putting a bunch
of shit in the backyard to block a UFO from landing, like lawn
chairs and an old washing machine and stuff. But my bitch mom
keeps putting it all back in the garage.

Later on, I read this article about cars and I get into it,
but after a few paragraphs I realize it's trying to trick me
into learning something. So I get mad
and throw it down. And now the Black
News is on TV. I HATE THE BLACK NEWS.
Derek Wood should be alive, romanc-
ing thirty-five year olds and perusing
his dream of becoming a Realtor. But
he's not.

PSYCHIC

THOUGHT

*Sagittarius: A past
struggle with a
goat may come to
mind when buying
a new car. Don't be
afraid to use that
knowledge.*

I remember once when I was over at Derek's house, he pointed to a big red spot on his bed and said, "That's from a chick's period." I was like, whoa.

Sometimes you don't know someone's gone until they've already left. Remember the time he went to juvie for a week for showing his dick to Cindy Gold's dog?

He will be missed dearly.

Then, out of nowhere, my bitch mom starts yelling at me to vacuum the living room and I almost go fucking berserk. I tell her I would fucking do it later, but she still keeps nagging.

So I go downstairs to do it, and my mom starts screaming at me, "What are you doing?" I scream back, "I'm throwing this bag out!" And she screams, "Get that bag outside!" And then I scream, "I AM!" If she knew I had the capability of letting a full-grown turkey into the house and giving it permission to tear apart her clothes, she would treat me with a lot more respect.

Once you reach a certain age, your parents can't do shit.

Word.

When I go outside, I punch the trash bag into the trash can and I hear my fat neighbor yelling, "Holy crap!" and then right after that, his wife yells, "Ouch." So there has to be

a one-to-one ratio for every "holy crap" per pelvic thrust.
My neighbor and his wife both weigh over five hundred pounds
each. When fat people make love, nobody knows whose boob is
whose.

Yeah, but the best thing about being married is that you don't have to wear a condom. That way, you know the girl doesn't have _herpes_.

What if she gets pregnant?

Have her ride on top. That way all the sperm will fall out. But if you forget and she does get pregnant, RUN. No, seriously, run. Get a motel room. Start a new life somewhere else. Just get out of there.

As I walk back in the garage, I stop and look at the floor,
and I see this weird-ass outline there. It's way bigger than
somebody's shoe. And it seems almost aquatic. Now that I think
about it, I'm pretty sure it's a flipper print that does not
conform to any of our classical zoological classifications.
Something was dropped on the floor, maybe a knife or food
wrapper, I don't know, and some weird-ass being went down and
scooped it up with a bare-naked flipper.

And then, I look up and see a pigeon with its head twisted
all the way off. Hillbillies are near, I know it. Quickly, I
go into fighting stance.

And there, near Jeff Trenton's sidewalk, I see the really
old guy whom Derek met at the grocery store—the hillbilly
who got hit in the face by the alien flipper. When the really
old guy sees me charging at him with my bow staff, he starts
running hard. I fucking start booking down the street and
push him into the bushes before he can do anything. He smells
like old chicken noodle soup.

He turns around real quick and just starts barfing all over
the bushes. I roll him over and I ask him if he's a hillbilly.
He doesn't say a word. Immediately, I realize he had received

training on how to resist interrogation. So I ask him again
and pinch his titty HARD. He quickly screams, "YEAH." So I
say, "Prove it." And he goes, "Whenever me and my buddies go
hang out, one of us ends up in the river, and before you know
it, we're all in there with him." I search his mind/beard,
and he's telling the truth.

BEARD MOVEMENT LIE DETECTION
(BEARD ACCESSING CUES)

WIGGLE UP/RIGHT
CONSTRUCTING **A VISUAL IMAGE:**
LYING

WIGGLE UP/LEFT
REMEMBERING **A VISUAL MEMORY:**
TELLING THE TRUTH

WIGGLE RIGHT
CONSTRUCTING
AN AUDITORY IMPRESSION:
LYING

WIGGLE LEFT
REMEMBERING
AN AUDITORY MEMORY:
TELLING THE TRUTH

WIGGLE DOWN/RIGHT
THINKING **KENISTHETIC/**
TACTILE SENSATION:
LYING OR **TELLING THE TRUTH**
DEPENDING ON THE CONTEXT

WIGGLE DOWN/LEFT
CRAVING DICK-SHAPED CRACKERS

This technique is not perfect though. The worst thing about
the Beard Movement Lie Detection Method is that if the guy
doesn't have a beard, you're fucked.

13:

Hillbilly Interrogation

12:09 p.m. EST. We walk over toward Walters Lake and sit. I ask the really old guy about his childhood, and he says being a hillbilly, he didn't have much. When he was a little hillbilly his only toy was a potato and his mom ate it one morning. I say his mom was a dick for doing that. He agrees. Then I tell him about my bitch mom, and her telling me to throw out a trash bag when I WAS ALREADY DOING IT, which was bullshit. We both get really mad. And then we laugh. But then, we think about it more deeply, and then get REALLY REALLY mad. I'm going to rip up a couple of her blouses when I get home this afternoon for sure.

I ask him about what Dead Derek Wood said—the aliens and the forest and stuff. He refuses at first, but I pinch his titty again, and he immediately continues the story from where Dead Derek left off.

"After the alien slapped me, I was pretty pissed off. I pretended that I was passed out, but I wasn't. I closed my eyes but still looked through my eyelashes, and that's when I saw some messed-up shit. Another alien came out of the ship, and his flippers were HUGE. Probably the leader. Everybody there

stopped what they were doing. And smoke was everywhere. I got
scared/angry. Then he walked right past me, real slow, with
his flippers squiggling in the moonlight. He went over to the
other guy who got hit with the rock. I couldn't see what he
was doing, but one of the other aliens, with smaller flippers,
was hitting a tree with a stick as hard as he could for over
ten minutes. Then he dropped the stick and walked away *like
it was nothing.* And that's when I really did pass out. When
I woke up, I felt my cheek."

I ask if I could see it—where the flipper hit him. He
lifts up his beard. And there, I see one man's entire meal
history in thirty-six square inches of hair. Green peppers,
almonds, chicken nuggets. The hairs part, and there it is—the
scratch.

I am standing on the precipice of a great Void. At this
moment, for the first time ever, I know what it is like
to BE a beard—the fractured state of being many hairs,
yet one entity. I look at the beard, and, for a moment,
the beard looks at me. Then, out of nowhere, my right
eardrum fills up with jelly. There's an electric popping
sound coming from somewhere. I look around.

The really old guy is gone.

There used to be this guy Brian. He didn't change
his shoes after work. So they always smelled like
pepperonis, and he always got chased by dogs. I wonder
whatever happened to him . . .

I think I'm somewhere else.

14:

D u d e ,   W h a t   t h e   F u c k

DUDE, I just traveled to a place where time
meant nothing, or at least it didn't mean much. Whatever happened, whatever I saw, it was definitely another dimension,
or some weird-ass house.

But I don't remember what the hell happened, and what I do
remember I can't begin to understand. Imagine the weirdest
thing you've ever seen—maybe some dude sneezing into his
hands, and then pulling out a snot web and screaming. Now
multiply that by about a billion. Only then will you have a
glimpse of what I'm talking about.

The only thing I do know is that something was implanted
in my brain, but I don't know what. Regardless, one has to
wonder whether my inability to remember the incident was due
to either short-term memory loss or a deliberate effort by
the Hot Pocket itself to block my recall.

*You mean Dead Derek's Hot
Pocket was consciously doing this?*

I DON'T KNOW, DUDE! All I know is that I smelled pepperonis all over the fucking place when I crossed the space/time
barrier.

These guys have to be
breaking some intergalactic law that I'm not
familiar with at the moment.

All right, listen, just because these aliens/ghosts may have
the ability to travel through space/time, doesn't mean that
they are brilliant/talented.

They could be like us.

That means we got a chance.

They probably haven't even
transcended their own egos.

Exactly. Now, I know that few intellectuals are talented
enough or willing to risk their academic reputations on going
over to another dimension and beating an entity's ass. But,
fuck it, I'll do it. There's no way they would expect us coming over there and messing up their homes and fighting a few
of them. Plus, we could get Derek back.

OK, Mike, I got the most important/intimate question anybody
might ever ask you. Would you go to another dimension, if some
dude came up to you and got right in your face and asked you
to go, but said you couldn't come back?

If that very dude could guarantee that everything would be paid for, then definitely.

And would you bring Shannon?

No. She couldn't handle it. When I took her to Kentucky she was bitching the WHOLE TIME.

Good. The mission is going to be difficult, and I don't want to end up just floating around for eons if we screw up. So let's gather all the stuff we know about interdimensional portals so far.

P S Y C H I C   T H O U G H T

Scorpio: If you continue to let a certain person call you "Cow Pie," then it will shape your life in such a way that your entire existence will be punctuated by a certain air of la vie ambigue. Also, beware of hairless people.

IMPORTANT/CAUTION

Everybody will have their own reasons why they're messing with this stuff. Maybe you're just curious or a complete moron. Whichever it is, it doesn't matter. The point is that whatever your feelings are on such matters, it is important to address them honestly before going any further.

Many people have opened up a portal and tried to befriend a ghost to feed off its power. I have heard testimony of such attempts, and it's disgusting. If you don't mind having diarrhea cascading against your chest, I'd say go ahead. Otherwise, don't befriend a ghost/alien in general, or mess with opening portals specifically.

It's one thing to hear about ghosts and aliens in the papers or in the movies. It's quite another to have one lay a log right on your back.

Regardless of me and Mike Stevens's warning, many may still open an interdimensional portal and try to invoke a demon. It's stupid, I know, but there are many like that. If you do invoke a demon, the first thing you should know is to *never challenge* it. Big mistake. Maybe if you were skilled in the occult, you could defend yourself adequately. But few are. I know Mike doesn't even like me to talk about this because it encourages people.

Number one, it's against the law, Satanism or whatever.

Number two, you're endangering yourself and pretty much all your amigos.

If a demon is busy, which is usually the case, the demon may get back to you at a later time, usually within two to three business days. For someone who is NOT well-versed in quantum physics, it is strongly advised not to even talk to one.

Parker Brothers needs to change the recommended age for Ouija boards to thirty years old and up. Seriously.

Milton Bradley Ouija boards tend not to work, but the Parker Brothers ones are the most powerful. <u>It's an ancient relic, not a toy</u>.[18]

No stores in Bulgaria will sell them.

Last year, I borrowed a Ouija board from Scott Nichols to use with Ed Trimmel. We waited till dark and went to the cemetery with it. When we got there, we asked if any spirits wanted to talk. The pointer moved to NO, and we just started running.

One time, my friend accidentally contacted Satan and burnt his eyebrows off.

Plus, the chance of possession is very high. If someone gets possessed by a demon, his/her strength is multiplied ten times or more. What do you do if your friend gets possessed? Think about this. How does a one hundred forty-pound priest take down an eleven-year-old who is possessed by a demon? If the priest were to study jujitsu, he could put her in a triangle choke and then body slam the girl onto the ground, no problem. Believe it or not I actually KNOW a professional exorcist (my aunt's boyfriend). He's a 3rd dan in aikido. Pretty cool guy.

---

[18]Ouija boards have been around for hundreds of years. People only found out about it when some dude robbed the Vatican in the fourteenth century. The guy broke in and just started grabbing stuff without even knowing what he had.

AKIDO REQUIRED

About two years ago I was on a pagan chat board discussing this very subject. I told them not to do it. One lady was like, "I don't care." Well, guess what. Once you've contacted a demon, you're with it for life. That woman wittingly made contact last year, and *she'll never be able to wear a thong bikini again.*

People think I'm overly cautious about this stuff, but I am quite familiar with the Dark Arts. I was even initiated into a coven once. During one of the gatherings, one guy chopped his finger off, and we all had a bite. A couple weeks later, I tried a little bit of arm, and part of a toe. Everything was going well till the night one of the other members was up on a balcony, and spit on my hair and chanted, "Titty, titty, titty." It was then that I realized that I was in too deep, and it was time to get out. I left all of that behind long ago. Better stop there because if I keep going, my life may be in danger.

Mike, I'm surprised you never mentioned this before.

We are different people throughout our lives.

15:

P o r t a l s

CLUES:

* Found a flipper
  print

* Met the old
  hillbilly and he
  said the Boss Alien
  had huge flippers

ʌ Saw proof—scratch

* Went to another
  dimension, and
  got freaked out

* It smelled like
  pepperonis all
  over the place
  when I got there

OUR investigation has now
taken the inevitable turn from searching for a missing person to opening up
a portal to another dimension. So now,
in addition to investigating for more
clues in the Mortal Realm, we will be
dedicating our resources to transcend-
ing the boundaries of space/time to
access the Immortal Realm.

BASIC PORTAL
STRUCTURE

Now, most people have heard that
South Dakota is a state, one of the
United States of America. Most people,
including those who live *right next* to
South Dakota, accept that statement as
a fact. But check this out. I've got

sensitive information that Utah, Wyoming, Delaware, and one
or even both of the Dakotas ARE NOT real states, and are most
likely *giant portals*. You NEVER hear anything about those
states, or meet people from there.

I've been to Delaware before.
It sucks, but it's a real state.

OK, but have you been to the others?

No.

So you see my point.
And I heard if you take ONE wrong turn in Indiana you somehow end right back in Ohio or maybe even Wisconsin. Those
portals open when there is a lot of magnetic activity caused
by concentrated sonic vibrations.

Hawaii seems like it is a
very magnetic island too.

If it even exists . . .

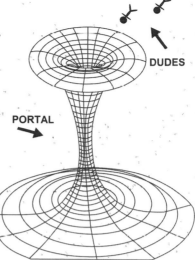

DUDES

PORTAL

There is even documented evidence[19] of a dude who teleported himself to a different space/time and everybody there was like, *Who the hell are you?*. The guy somehow managed to teleport himself back and supposedly there was a huge party afterward, but nobody knows for sure. So it definitely is possible.

> My friend's uncle opened a portal/interdimensional gateway a couple weeks ago, and now he's pretty pissed. (He's the type of guy who buys name-brand kitty litter.) What happened was, he was messing around in the garage with a bunch of Latin phrases/electronics and somehow opened up a gate/portal. The whole house went BERSERK. He couldn't banish the ghosts/aliens AT ALL. The only way he knows of to close it is to go into the original room and have the original person/people doing the original thing/stuff. BUT the problem is he can't meet the conditions!

Damn. That's definitely something we should consider before embarking on this shit. We need some backup.

---

[19]"Tipo extraño asoma de la nada." *La Jornada*, 19 Febrero 1914, ed. de la tarde: All. *Translation:* "Weird-Ass Dude Just Shows Up Out of Nowhere." *La Jornada*, 19 February 1914, late ed.: All.

Trey Hamburger
681 Lake George Road
Leonard, MI 48367

March 11, 2008

Professor Timothyq Arnoldsq
Harvardq Universityq
Physicsq Buildingq
17 Oxford Street
Cambridge, MA 02138

Dear Professor Timothyq Arnoldsq,

All right, I've written to a lot of people so far, and
got nothing. So just hear us out before you start judging
us.
   Now, listen, your name has been recommended to me
regarding interdimensional portals. My associate Mike
Stevens and I are very interested in your research and
would like very much to know more.
   So here it is.
   Yesterday I went to another dimension, and Mike Stevens
and I want to go back. I am not scared of ghosts/aliens
or other similar beings if things go wrong. And I know
that a lot of people may ask you about this sort of
thing, and you have to turn them down because you think
they couldn't handle it. Well, me and Mike have been
dealing with transdimensional beings for almost a week,
and we're the last people who would want to cause an
intergalactic "incident." We can handle this. *Plus, they
got Derek.*
   Oh, and don't think that I am totally careless about
this kind of thing. I have a stern seriousness about this
portal stuff because every time I think about it or talk
about it, I start shivering and get a cold feeling on
the back of my neck, if that's any indication. (It is.)
And there are some things I refuse to mess with—warlocks
being one of them. I was at this house once, and somebody
there said that we were "partying with a warlock." I
immediately left without saying bye to anyone.
   If you want to assist us, that's cool. But if you don't,
remember this: There must have been a time when you needed
help. Maybe you wanted a haircut really bad and nobody
wanted to give you one because everyone was just relaxing
at that very moment. But you were like, "Dude, come on."
And one dude got right in your face and was like, "Let it
go." But you still kept at it, and eventually it happened.

Sincerely,
Trey Hamburger, local scientist

P.S. If you don't understand what I'm talking about,
please burn this letter.

Trey Hamburger
681 Lake George Road
Leonard, MI 48367

March 21, 2008

Mr. Hamburger,

This letter is in response to your March 11 inquiry
regarding "opening a portal." Mr. Hamburger, I'm not
exactly sure what you're talking about. First, what
do you mean by "portal"? Do you mean a wormhole, or a
hole in space that connects to another place in space-
time? (1) The existence of any physical manifestations
of wormholes is merely theoretical and, at best,
mathematically possible. (2) If wormholes were proven to
exist and you were able to open one, these features of
space-time are far too unstable for people to traverse
with any foreseeable technology. And finally, (3) there
are a lot of very smart people working on this problem,
and as of yet there is still no solution. I would be
quite surprised if this field could be furthered by the
work of two guys messing around in their basement. I
suggest going to your library and educating yourself on
the matter.
    As for your feelings about warlocks, I cannot bring
myself to care less.

Guy

Damn, dude, we need a major breakthrough, bad.

16:

Major Shit/
Breakthrough

MIKE comes over and says his cousin just told him some major shit.

Dude, my cousin just told me some major shit.

Dude, what?

It's forbidden to even speak of it.

Dude.

OK, listen. There is this mysterious cave in Leonard that contains some markings by dudes unknown, and those markings speak of a legend/prophecy.

Japanese geologists found the cave/legend/prophecy a couple years ago, but took a vow of secrecy because they were afraid of regular dudes hearing about it, <u>thinking it was about them</u>, and basically trying to fulfill it. You know—running around town ripping off people's wigs, pole-vaulting through windows—stuff like that. I only know about it because my cousin knows one of the guys.

The whole thing basically states that a couple thousand years ago, there was this guy who was cool. He had a base and several dudes who backed him up. But then out of nowhere, some messed-up shit went down, and the main guy went into <u>combat mode</u>, BIG-TIME. This main guy had a huge cellar full of weaponry and he called up the most intense dudes he knew. They went through the countryside beating the crap out of ghosts and aliens and warlocks. There is even a story where the main guy saw a this alien walking down the street and he shot a crossbow right through its head, and all this juice was squirting all over the place and a bystander who saw everything freaked out and just started puking everywhere. It was sick. But the main guy was like, Dude. Chill. And the dude chilled.

Damn, dude. This totally validates a lot of the feelings I've been having lately.

Yeah, and throughout the cave, there were all these stories about all these really intense dudes defending the Earth from all these ghosts/aliens. But near the bottom, there was a particular story about how one day, in the future, something is going to happen again, and many will puke, and some dude will be chosen to go haywire and just start whaling on interdimensional beings again.

A chosen dude will come forward.

Yeah, the prophecy says that this Chosen Dude will foresee some major shit, but the townspeople will be like, "Dude, you're a moron." And the Chosen Dude will be like, "Shut up." But they won't.

That just happened yesterday.

BUT, my cousin warned me that until that day, people have to shut up about this legend because of the ramifications of some idiot hearing about it and thinking it was him and then pretty much screwing everything up BIG TIME.

DUDE, WHO EXACTLY IS THIS CHOSEN DUDE?

Nobody Knows who it is, except that it's just some guy.

That sounds like me. Here's what's weirder. I have type-O blood, which is supposed to be pure blood. Man, it's a good thing this whole legend thing is happening because I totally expected to be working in retail next week.

So do you think you're the one?

Yeah, probably.

There is a catch though. If the WRONG DUDE comes forward and flips out and takes it upon himself to fulfill the legend/prophecy, and mess some shit up hard, he will bring with him the APOCALYPSE—The End of the World as We Know It. Are you still willing to do this if it means bringing about the demise of EVERYTHING?

Dude, if it means that we might become billionaires and get hand jobs from famous people, then the possibility of a full-scale apocalypse is worth it.

All right, before I embrace the title of the Chosen Dude, I have to clear something up, BIG TIME. OK, Josh Marshall, if you're reading this, I have to talk to you about something which may have disturbed you. Do you remember yesterday at Ed Trimmel's house, when you walked into the bathroom and saw me with my pants around my ankles, softly smacking my crotch? I just want to let you know that I was IN NO WAY jerking off. Let me explain. *Five minutes prior to the incident*, I had slipped and fallen onto a beehive. Although I had suffered not one bee sting as you may have noticed, unbeknownst to me, a single bee burrowed itself through my jeans and underwear. When I had realized this, like any other regular/normal person would, I immediately went to the bathroom and attempted to coax the bee away from my balls *without angering it*, by softly stroking outward at a steady and deliberate pace. NOW LOOK. Seriously. If someone were falsely accused of jerking off two days prior, wouldn't you think that person would TAKE EVERY PRECAUTION not be accused of jacking off for the next few days or so? Someone would have to be the dumbest person on the planet to take a chance like that again. In conclusion, I hope this sufficiently resolves the matter, or at least satisfies your curiosity enough to put the matter to rest <u>for good</u>.

Nobody needs to talk about this again. It's over.

17:

A New Mission

DAMN. What started out as a simple case of a teleporting Hot Pocket has turned into a mission that will decide the fate of the entire universe, or at least the town of Leonard. Mike and I watch TV for a couple hours to calm down. Then, out of nowhere, the damn gurgle noise gurgles. Pop flies all over the couch, and we just start running. We come back up from the basement ten minutes later, pissed off.

Right then, Mike and I make a blood pact, vowing to fulfill the prophecy and complete this mission even if it means we might die and never, ever get the chance to put it in a woman's butt. I don't even want to think about that possibility—but it's there, and we totally recognize the risk.

If there is some way, I mean I know it's a long shot, but if it happens and we figure out what's going on and maybe even stop it, then I think people should start calling me THE HAWK, or just HAWK.

FUCK YEAH. Let's do this.

We'll be like these renowned scientists, totally respected by the intellectual community BUT ALSO by gang members too because they'll know we've been through a lot.

Now we prepare.

While waiting for the specific Latin phrases and/or electronic schematics from Professor Timothyq Arnoldsq (if he ever changes his mind), me and Mike Stevens get a shitload of steak knives from Jeff Trenton's house. His parents are pretty much alcoholics and wouldn't notice anyway.

We now begin the formation of a group of the most intense dudes alive.

3.

AN ELITE
FIGHTING FORCE

<u>WARNING:</u>
REALLY INTENSE DUDES
ONLY AFTER THIS POINT

Trey Hamburger
681 Lake George Road
Leonard, MI 48367

March 12, 2008

Public Communications and Inquiries Management Office
NASA Headquarters
Suite 5K39
Washington, DC 20546-0001

Dear NASA,

JUST LISTEN. I got one request and could one of you
guys at least think about it first before you say no?
Now, here it is. I would like to submit my name into
the application tub of future fighter pilots against a
UFO invasion. If there is no such force yet, then let
me suggest that me and Mike Stevens start one. Because
the question isn't anymore, *Can they even get here?* The
question is, *When are they coming and how BAD are we going to
beat their ass when they do?*
   Here are some of the things I would like to focus on.

   i. piloting skills and improving our ability to maneuver
     quicker than ever before
  ii. more high-energy laser cannons on each plane
 iii. recruiting guys who don't give a crap, and are ready
     for whipping around in a space jet, no problem

The recruits shouldn't have families or codependent
girlfriends because these guys will think twice about
flying right into a UFO if they have to. (I could do
it, but most people couldn't.) In addition to that, they
should have the following qualities:

  1. Be ready for when some shit goes down.
  2. Can't tell anyone where the main base is at.
  3. Be OK with looking out of a space ship window for
     extended periods of time.
  4. Be able to understand that they're part of an Inner
     Circle.
  5. Cannot lie IN ANY WAY to other members.
  6. Can pretty much back up whatever they say (this may
     seem obvious, but there are a lot of morons out
     there).
  7. Be regular guys who are pretty cool to hang out with
     because they'll basically have to train together for
     months at a time. Plus they'll have to get along
     while on missions and while partying their asses off
     during the down time.

and

8. *Be willing to relocate anywhere in the solar system.*

That's just a start. But don't worry, if you put me on this Secret Team of Elite Fighters, I won't tell ANYBODY. People might come up to me and ask what I've been up to, and I'll just stare blankly, *giving them nothing*.

Your new Squadron Leader,
Trey Hamburger

P.S. If you don't have any plans for destroying these creatures, then I would like you to consider me for a diplomatic position. Or, if you guys need any help or somebody to experiment on in exchange for a small stipend, then I'm your man.

SO FAR NO REPLY

Buttholes.

WEDNESDAY

18:

The "Indian" Again

AT 4:18 p.m. EST, we have a major breakthrough in the investigation. The "Indian" makes its first move since Mike threw her's at it. Todd "Semen" Niemen calls up and says it was at the grocery store late last night and bought a box of Wheat Thins.

Are you fucking serious?

Yup.

Did you know Nabisco is owned by al-Qaeda?

Yup.

This is way bigger than we ever thought. Nabisco also has the patent for flying saucer technology. AND THAT'S FUCKING BULLSHIT. That shit should be available to everyone, or at least not be a fucking secret.[20] We need to set up twenty-four-hour surveillance of the "Indian." That way we'll be able to witness everything that goes on there.

Sheep noises. Possible strangulation. Whatever.

Mike and I set up camp in the bushes near the "Indian" habitat.

5:12 p.m. EST

The "Indian" guy gets home from work and gets the mail, but he does so in a way that indicates he may have sacrificed somebody the night before. Mike and I are furious.

5:50 p.m. EST Jeff Trenton joins the group.[21] Brings a nail gun. Redeems himself.

5:51 p.m. EST We ask Jeff Trenton to place cinnamon-scented pillows on the "Indian's" porch in an effort to induce his tongue to explode.[22] Jeff understands the gravitas of our request and promptly agrees.

---

[20]We confront Nabisco about this and, to this date, they have never said a word. See **Exhibit H:** *Letter to Nabisco* for details.

[21]Although Jeff Trenton has constantly expressed his fealty to me, I've become suspicious of him in the last couple days. When I was over at his house, he was eating a donut, and I asked him if he had any more. He paused for a moment and said no. He then changed the subject quickly and went toward an open cupboard. I watched closely without being obvious. Before he closed the cupboard door I could see a near full box of donuts in there. There could be more to this.

[22]*Quarterly Journal of Nonnegligible Allergen Reactions,* fall 1907, issue 5. "A Comprehensive List of the Most Dangerous Pillows Ever," p. 31-45.

IMPORTANT NOTE REGARDING SPYING:

I would suggest that all ladies be VERY CAREFUL about sunbathing nude in your backyard. I talked to a guy in the U.S. Navy who worked at the National Geospatial Satellite Intelligence Agency—I don't know exactly what his job position was, he was never allowed to say—but he told me that in the main office there is a giant bulletin board containing satellite pictures of women's beavers.

The government has a "black budget" for this kind of thing.

5:52 p.m. EST Jeff Trenton crawls on his stomach and reaches over the porch to carefully place the pillow near the door. Although he isn't seen, Jeff violently rolls back to us.

6:00 p.m. EST The pillow is still on the porch. There is little movement inside the "Indian's" habitat. We wait patiently.

6:08 p.m. EST Todd "Semen" Niemen crawls near the porch to better position the pillow for maximum visibility. Then, out of nowhere, the "Indian" opens the door. With a tone that betrays a venomous passion for murder and death and a corresponding buildup of lactic acid, the "Indian" says, "Yo." We run.

Lactic acid is also produced commercially for use in pharmaceuticals, some food products, leather tanning, and textile dyeing.

6:09 p.m. EST While running, tragedy strikes when a pigeon flies into Jeff Trenton's head and briefly knocks him out. Later, after all is finished, we hunt pigeons in anger.

CLOSE COMBAT FIGHTING TECHNIQUES

LEARN KARATE

Most extraterrestrials are masters of
tae kwon do and jujitsu. So you need to
get in and get out quickly, inflicting
the most damage and incapacitating them
in the fewest moves possible—trust me,
you don't want to have a drawn-out fight
with these beings.

First off, there's no reason that a
person shouldn't invest in learning martial arts if they're serious about fighting ghosts/aliens. If there aren't any
grandmasters close enough to your house,
then I can go over a few moves and possible scenarios to use them in.

ATTITUDE

Fighting is all about your attitude. There are people
who have beaten up tigers or leopards because they were
mad enough. Going buck wild always wins. If you saw some
guy, lying on his stomach doing a puzzle, you'd probably assume you could beat his ass easily. But if that
same guy were ripping up the puzzle and clawing at the
carpet, you probably wouldn't even say hi. Adopt a similar approach. To most people this may seem like a small
thing. But those who have been in combat will know how
practical this is.

MAINTAIN EYE CONTACT

SPECIFIC SCENARIOS

Now, with that attitude in mind, I will go over a few
scenarios you may find yourself in. Things may get complicated quickly and you need to have a realistic template
to work from when you are attacked.

I can retract my gonads into my body if I have to.

SCENARIO 1

You and your friends are well-armed, with plenty of ammunition.
You guys are walking around the forest looking for a dog, and
you discover a crashed UFO. The landing has fractured the hull,
popping open the hatches and windows. There is still some smoke
coming out of the openings, and you can see one of the beings
looking out the window. What do you do?

Suggested Response

A. Carefully watch them while hiding in shrubs. If the
beings are roaming around outside, wait till they all
go inside the craft. Then board the ship and kill or
capture the crew, regardless of the consequences. After
that, play it by ear.
        or
B. Immediately start shooting, and then stab into the
open hatches with a bayonet. Then wrap it up with some
pepper spray and dynamite. After that, go home and
chill.

SCENARIO 2

OK, you suffer an alien abduction. You are armed. But you have
no idea where you are, or how many aliens are on board. You
have not been anesthetized yet. There are no other amigos you
are aware of on board.

Suggested Response

There is a time and place for an offensive posture. This
is that time and place. If the crew is smaller than you
and it's possible to hijack the ship, you should probably
do that. If they do have guns, immediately start thinking about nachos to confuse them (see *Full Specifications
Regarding Ghosts/Aliens*), and while they're in a daze,
begin firing and make your way toward the exit. When you
get home, chill.

SCENARIO 3

You're in your backyard, chillin' with a couple of friends.
You're not armed this time. Out of nowhere, this alien busts

out of the bushes, looks right at you, and starts walking over
real slow.

Suggested Response

Look him in the eyes, and talk in a monotone voice. Say,
"Don't worry, amigo, I'm not going to attack you." THEN
ATTACK. This is Black Ops stuff. Nobody expects somebody
to attack right after they calmly state that they're not
going to. Ask any high-level martial artist if you don't
believe me. This technique is very similar to the egg-
question-then-thrust-sword move.

I've tasted human blood before.

Some may be appalled at the suggestion that we must
revert to the brutality of cave people just to live. But
you have to realize that when you're dealing with beings
that are willing to travel light-years just to make a
sock levitate,[23] there is no room for any scruple or com-
punction about the methods used.

NOTE: There's something about constant combat that
can drive you insane. So don't be trying this stuff
out every time you go to a party. You're liable to
go somewhere in your mind you can't come back from.
Plus, people will stop inviting you places.

[23]Josh Evans's house, October 2, 2007, 1:09 a.m.

SIMPLE POINTS
TO REMEMBER

- A head butt is probably the highest percentage one-shot knockout strike. It is extremely useful in fights, especially in other dimensions, where no one expects them.

- Most "fights" are won before they begin, and aggressors will back down if you maintain eye contact and are not intimidated by them. So if some alien starts staring at you, stare right back.

- Learn how to go from zero to violent whenever you hear something messed up.

- Work on your sprints.

- Use anything.

Utensils, Motherfucker!

CONCLUSION

So remember, when you're watching TV, they could be up in their spaceships doing crunches and pull-ups. So be prepared.[24]

EMERGENCY ALERT:

HOLY SHIT. Mike and I stumble upon something that may shake the very foundations of everything we know about the dudes we hang out with.

We have reason to believe that Ed Trimmel was hatched.

[24]For a suggested home workout routine, see **Exhibit E:** *Daily Workout Schedule.*

19:

An Elite Fighting Force of Dudes

OK, Ed Trimmel is just a regular dude. He wasn't hatched.

He just said something about eggs that, at the time, appeared VERY suspicious.

CLUES:

* We discover an ancient prophecy about a dude who will whale on ghosts/aliens. I'm probably that dude.

* The "Indian" likes Wheat Thins.

And he yelled at Mike for throwing rocks at birds.

If he didn't have a belly button, we would have beaten him.

Later that night we check the "Indian's" porch, *and the cinnamon-scented pillow is gone.* In light of current developments and the recent "Indian" attack, Mike and I begin recruiting for our Elite Fighting Force of Dudes. That way, when it retaliates, we'll be ready.

For those of you who want to join the force, I have written below a simple guide of what to bring and what it will be like to be a part of an Elite Fighting Force.

IMPORTANT NOTE:

If you know a dude, and he's cool, but wonder if you should invite him to join up, watch how he responds *after he drops some food on his shirt.* If he freaks out and gets all pissed off, don't let him join up. If he's pretty chill about it, he's ready.

BECOMING AN ELITE FIGHTING FORCE
TEAM MEMBER

Before you even show up, please note that your mere presence at Mike Stevens's backyard constitutes an automatic waiver of liability. By just being there, you agree that you cannot, and will not, hold Trey Hamburger, Mike Stevens, Todd "Semen" Niemen, Jeff Trenton, or anyone we hang out with liable for injury, harm, or anxiety that may befall you while at the training grounds, shooting range, or anywhere on the property. If you disagree with this automatic waiver of liability, please indicate so by being a diaper baby and not showing up.

YEAH. DIAPER BABIES.

BUT if you do show up, it is important to remember that you
are invited guests, so don't mess up any of Mike's mom's flow-
erbeds when performing moves. Such actions may result in us
having to find a new base. Or if at any time and for any reason
you start judging us or acting like you're better than us, you
may be instructed to leave by the landowner or his appointee.

ELITE FIGHTING FORCE ITINERARY

- The first day of practice will consist of everyone
  getting to know each other and showing each other moves
  we know.
- The second day, we'll start looking for beings to fight,
  and then we find them and proceed to fight them.
- The third day's itinerary is open to suggestion.

Not many people can keep up the intense attitude to success-
fully execute their role. So we expect only the most dedicated
to stay with the team. But remember no one shall be compelled
to participate in a conflict that he or she cannot fully and
willfully support in his or her heart. No one shall be FORCED
to fight a ghost or alien. You have to want to do it.

Officially our unit does not
exist. So don't go around telling people about
it, unless you think they could handle it.

BASIC EQUIPMENT TO BRING

1. First-aid kit
2. Sleeping bag
3. Anything that can be used as a weapon (knives, bow staffs, chains, whatever)
4. Construction paper and scissors for logos
5. Potato chips
6. Pop
7. Copy of the U.S. Constitution
8. Claw hammer

SECOND THOUGHTS?

If you're still wondering whether you should come the first day, ask yourself these questions:

- Could I abandon a mission without shooting anything?
- Am I a little diaper baby?
- Have I shat the bed in the last six months? If yes, did I do it because I felt a desire for punishment? Or because I was just dreaming that I was sitting on a toilet? (If the latter, don't worry about this one.)
- Would I ever sympathize with a ghost or an alien?
- Do I get heart attacks easily?
- Am I incapable of killing?

If you answered yes to any of these questions, you are unfit for service. Although you can still hang out if you're cool.

No weapons training though. Seriously.

We have our meetings every night at 8 p.m. at Louie's, right near the outskirts of Leonard. When you get to Louie's, tell the waitress you are with the CONCERNED CITIZENS meeting. She'll know where to point you. You need NOT mention anything about ghosts, aliens, or broadswords. Only a few people could accept the existence of ghosts/aliens as fact and not lose their capability of living happy, meaningful lives. In other words, *it's a little too intense to talk about.*

For our country's sake, I hope that no one who trained under us ever goes bad.

IMPORTANT POINTS TO REMEMBER

1. *Don't be a dick.*
We do not advocate overt acts of violence and/or aggression. If you go up to some dude who wasn't doing anything to you and just start whaling on him, don't expect us to back you up.
2. *Don't bring a beret.*
Many people wear berets. Nobody is going to prevent you from wearing a beret, but remember, it is TOTALLY USELESS. They do not shade your eyes from sun, wind, or rain, and they can become extremely hot. Unless you just want to look totally sweet, there is no reason to wear a beret. So don't wear one. This is about survival.[25]

I just spilled fruit salad all over my shirt, and I'm cool with it.

__YOU'RE READY.__

[25]If you want to start your own chapter of the Elite Fighting Force of Dudes, please see Mike Stevens's **Exhibit F:** *Starting Your Own Force* at the back of the book for a field guide on what to do.

TEAM MEMBER SECRET CODES

RECOGNITION SIGNALS:

a. *Visual:* Team members will be wearing their shirt collars up and will have an intense look.

b. *Verbal:* Team Member: "You ready to party?" Contact: "Maybe."

DANGER SIGNAL:

Team members, upon recognizing danger or mission compromise, will wink three times consecutively with right eye. Or if any member is wearing a T-shirt backward, it means to send reinforcements.

If scheduled meeting does not take place, chill.

---

681 Lake George Road
Leonard, MI 48367

March 12, 2008

Michigan Militia
P.O. Box 90846
Redford, MI 48240

Dear Michigan Militia,

OK, me and Mike Stevens have started our own group of really intense individuals, an Elite Fighting Force. Not surprisingly, your group and our group have some overlapping interests. You guys are into combat and basic weaponry. <u>So are we</u>. But we think you guys have failed to see one threat that Mike Stevens and I are fully aware of—ghosts/aliens. If you guys are interested in joining forces against this type of thing, we would totally be up for it.

Although me and Mike are not old enough to use guns, we do have swords and are trained in the Dark Arts. (We are budding psions.)

Thank you,
Trey Hamburger, Squadron Leader Class A
Mike Stevens, Squadron Leader Class B

P.S. Don't worry, for each mission we take on we have a quiet determination to get the job done, and will punctuate each success with a hard-core session of high fives.

NO REPLY

NO REPLY EITHER! WHAT THE FUCK? These are exactly the types of dudes who should understand and yet they don't.

I KNOW!

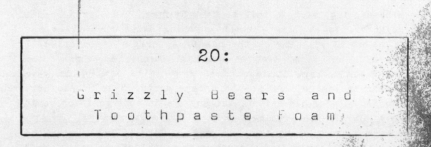

20:

Grizzly Bears and Toothpaste Foam

SOME guy shows up at a meeting for the Elite Fighting Force and says he wants to join up. We interrogate him, and he seems cool at first. But when it comes time for him to pass the loyalty test and let Mike Stevens shoot an arrow at his face, he abruptly leaves. Most people are not ready for the intensity of such specialization and the high degree of emotional release that goes along with joining an Elite Fighting Force of Dudes. (This has been a long-term problem for us that we can't seem to resolve.)

Later, after the meeting, Mike hears a gurgle near Derek Wood's house while riding his bike, and goes right off a bridge. The gurgling has become part of our lives now. While brushing my teeth, or making lunch, the gurgle is out there somewhere in the distance. It is a constant reminder of what we must accomplish. Many may feel we have become hasty in our training protocol, but they must understand that it is because of the nature of our enemy.

GURGLE CLUES

Mike and I go over to talk to Mark Stenner, Dead Derek Wood's neighbor, to see if he knows anything about the gurgle, or if he heard anything on the night of Derek's evaporation. I knock on the door. Even though Mark Stenner is a respected community member, it is rumored that while camping he gave a grizzly bear a hand job to escape death. Many people have shunned him for his action, but anybody in that position would have done the same thing.

Mark Stenner opens the door and is like, "What's up?" And I'm like, "Derek's dead. Do you know anything?" He says, "No." And I'm like, "What's your past like?" And he's like, "I'm from Ohio." And I'm like, "Shit." And we leave.

Then Mike and I walk over and talk to Dead Derek's other neighbor, Justin Monroe. (He had an uncle in Des Moines, Iowa, that dealt in black market Christmas ornaments.) We ask him about the gurgle, if he's ever heard it. He has, but he gives us no new intelligence regarding its origin. BUT he does tell us some messed-up information about toothpaste. Like, you know when you brush your teeth and it makes all that foam in your mouth? I just found out that the foam <u>does not do anything</u>. It's just there to make people feel better, and THAT'S IT.

FUCK, man, if there was ever a time when I thought I didn't have to be suspicious, it was when I was brushing my fucking teeth!

Sorry, man. I had no idea that if we dug down this deep, we were going to regret it.

NO. It's better that I learn the truth than lead a deluded existence.

21:

Psychic Powers/Chi

PISSED about putting so much work into a false lead, Mike and I decide to prepare for our voyage to another dimension to find Derek Wood. So we focus on training our psychic powers. Even though some of us may not have fully developed our chi—

I haven't yet.

—we cannot proceed without a cursory understanding of the Dark Arts.

TRAINING YOUR PSYCHIC POWERS

W A R N I N G :

You are about to become aware of the unknown. You are about
to access energies that have never ever been accessed. You may
detect subtle energy changes. Depending on your sensitivity
level you may actually be able to CONTROL that energy. You have
been warned.

OK, there are definitely people out there who can use "chi"
to affect others, either in combat or for healing purposes.
For example, have you ever thought that something was going
to happen, and something, maybe something totally different,
actually did? Or you suddenly came up with the right words
for someone to emotionally open up and give you an HJ? If so,
then you might definitely have psychic powers.

I've seen people start speaking
with a British accent without ever having
studied the language.

You might be saying to yourself, "I've never met anyone who
can teleport or see the future, and I have met a lot of motherfuckers." Well listen to this. Just last month, a personal
friend of mine was about to take a job at a hardware store,
but for some reason his stomach went nuts and he didn't. THE
NEXT DAY THE STORE EXPLODED. Explain that.[26] And another time,
I complained about my English teacher, about what a moron she
was, and a couple days later she was in the hospital for two
months, getting her uterus taken out.

[26] As for me, I really don't even like talking about this, but I'm the most psychically powerful out of all of my friends. After smoking a little bit last week, I
was sitting down in a big overstuffed chair, and I had this intense experience of
becoming the chair. The thing is, only my eyes were visible. I imagined that if
anybody looked at me, all they would see is this big fat chair with two blinking
eyes. I don't know how, but I definitely think I could use this technique to escape
a battle if I'm low on energy and run out of peanuts or something. I told Todd
"Semen" Niemen about my ability, and now he wants it too. I don't know how to tell
him, but it's just too powerful. (You have to be careful who you talk to about this
stuff. I mean, a lot of people would abuse this gift.)

> *Sometimes, I have a vague feeling of having lived in Alabama.*

TELEPATHY

Now, let's say that we cross over to another dimension and for some reason, Mike, you get sent to a different space coordinate than I do. We'll have to contact each other so we can meet up in case our cell phones don't work in a different space/time. There is a way. Telepathy. You might even be saying, "Yo, I want this thing, but how do I tap into it?" OK, here it is. Let's say you really want some nachos and your amigo's got some. BUT you don't feel like being a dick about it and asking him, and then he's socially obligated to give you some. You feel needy, and he feels like he's missing out on a handful of nachos. OK, now listen. If you simply concentrate hard enough on the nachos *without saying a word*, he'll probably end up just giving you some. So (1) you won't feel like a dick, and (2) he'll feel all benevolent and shit because he thinks he did it "on his own."[27]

> *In many ways, our Earth-based language is insufficient to communicate what I want to say sometimes.*

We can use that same method if either of us gets into trouble and can't use our mouths for some interdimensional reason. If you're trapped in a bioslime cone, just concentrate on your fellow amigo, and a couple minutes later, he'll bust you out of it and feed you some peanuts if you're about to die. It's good that you're coming, Mike, because telepathy works best between people who hang out together.

---

[27]How the author learned telepathy is not important.

If I get a psychic message from somebody I don't know, I'm like, "Yeah, so?"

Me too. The best way to focus your energy is to plug your ears. You'll also notice that your sight will increase dramatically too, and vice versa. Some people even believe that babies are born with all their Lost Powers totally intact.

Psychic Babies

I just got chills from that.

There are dangers, though. I have heard stories of telekinesis gone out of control with people floating around, bumping into ceilings and getting smothered by curtains. Also there is a legend in our neighborhood that Jeff Trenton burst a cat's heart by merely staring at it. It's a technique that can paralyze anything that lives, whether it be animal or human. Regardless, whatever transpired between Jeff and that cat, *he went too far*. This kind of thing isn't for babies, psychic or not.

Now for a demonstration. Do you have any mysteries you need psychically solved? Cause I'll do it right now. Go ahead, give me a mystery. You got one?

OK, yeah, well my—

It's in a bag.

What's in a bag?

You'll know.

You have a Golden Gift.

PSYCHIC   THOUGHT

Aquarius: Although tempting, don't pursue the "Woman's Period" Topic when you meet with your neighbor next week. It will take you to a place so rife with horror that you may never wish to see a vagina on the Internet for several weeks.

ANIMAL BACKUP

There may come a time when you will look to an animal for backup in case your amigo goes flying over a cliff or gets sawed up during a mission. Ed Trimmel told us that when his grandma had a heart attack, her bird called 911 and basically saved her life. Here is a simple way to get a chicken/duck to do pretty much anything you want it to.

I hate it when birds are celebrated for having basic numerical competency. One of the biggest mistakes of pet owners is to sincerely believe that it was never about the food.

HOW TO SUCCESSFULLY HYPNOTIZE A CHICKEN/DUCK TO HELP OUT

Phase One: Unfold the wing.

Phase Two: Take the head and tuck it under the wing.

Phase Three: Swing it around in circles *slowly* at least fifteen times.

If done correctly, the chicken/duck will be fully hypnotized, and should stay like this for about five minutes—**the critical time.** During that period you can program it to basically do whatever you want it to. When you're finished, clap your hands to bring the chicken/duck to an alert state and ready for battle. After you have hypnotized and programmed a chicken/duck, one of the first questions will be, *Will this chicken/duck remember anything?* The answer is almost always no. (But be careful though, it's pretty easy to get lost in the sordid world of poultry magazines.)

You can do the same thing with trout/bass too, if necessary.

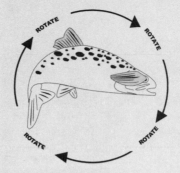

Trout Undergoing Phase Two of Animal Hypnotism

A duck would murder its own mother over a slice of bread. So don't trust them unless they're completely hypnotized.

Dude, what's your deal with birds? Why are you so hesitant about bringing ducks onto the team? And why are you so passionate about the human vs. bird intelligence gap?

I don't like to talk about it, and it took me many years before I could share this with another amigo. When I was younger, there used to be a goose that lived in the forest nearby. And whenever I would go outside, the goose would peek its head out of the bushes and watch me. At first I was cool with it. But then, a couple months later, they found a kid in that same forest who was completely sucked dry of blood. From then on I could feel that goose's hollow eyes against my back whenever I went outside. It started following me too. And even during those times when I would be having fun and forgot about that damn goose, I would hear a loud-ass honk in the distance. This state of panic went on for years until we moved to Leonard. I think we got out of there just in time. Since then, I have avoided towns with a high goose-population density. In fact, a couple years later my aunt let her guard down once at the beach, and a seagull dropped a log on her arm. She thought it was suntan lotion and smeared it all over. The incident might have been connected, but I don't know for sure. Regardless, never let that chirp fool you. With the constant huddling and quiet peeping, how could one NOT think these birds are up to something?

I thought I would never understand but, alas, I too am disgusted.

Trey Hamburger
681 Lake George Road
Leonard, MI 48367

March 11, 2008

Dr. Carroll Ames
Psychology Department
280 Armstrong Hall
Southern Michigan University
Ypsilanti, MI 48197

Dear Professor Dr. Carroll Ames,

Now it can be told. Over the past couple days I have
been conducting a scientific experiment here on you with
thought-transference (telepathy) messages and the results
are now in, and have been analyzed. I sent thought-
transference messages to you and a couple other people.
So far, no one responded.

Considering the content, if any of the subjects had
received my messages, I definitely think they would have
urgently contacted me. I mean, I was saying some weird
shit.

But to date, none has said a *word*.

So I must conclude that my experiment has failed. Man,
this is the kind of thing that will keep me up ALL night.
But, like, if you actually do get the message, *it would be
epic*. So it's definitely worth it. I'm going to try again
soon with some even weirder shit. So let me know if you
"get anything" in the next couple days in case my message
is late or something.

Thanks,
Trey Hamburger, sophomore

P.S. Is it OK to go into the hot tub whilst high?

SOUTHERN MICHIGAN
MICHIGAN'S TECHNICAL UNIVERSITY

Trey Hamburger
681 Lake George Road
Leonard, MI 48367

Mr. Trey Hamburger,

I have received your first and second letter regarding
psychic experimentation. So, as it seems, I suppose it
is necessary to supply a response. Neither I, nor anyone
else in the department, as far as I know, has been
receiving unsolicited psychic messages. If, in fact,
someone does come to my office suggesting that they have
been having thoughts about "weird shit" that may not
be their own, I will be sure to let you know. However,
due to the nature of my work and my lack of free time
thereof, it would be appreciated if you directed your
letters and thoughts elsewhere.
  Good luck with your experiment.

Thank you,
C.A.

NATIONAL FEDERATION OF RETARDED PEOPLE
Okalahoma

NFRP
1234 Retard Road
Stupid Idiot, OK 47362924

Dr. Carroll Ames
Psychology Department
280 Armstrong Hall
Southern Michigan University
Ypsilanti, MI 48197

Dear Carroll Ames,

Congratulations, YOU'RE IN.

Sorry,
Trey Hamburger, NOT the president

Trey Hamburger

Mike Stevens, also NOT the president

MIKE STEVENS

22:

Tuesday,
A New Title

WE just found out something that will definitely help us with our investigation. BIG-TIME. Plus this is a strong indication that I'm probably the Chosen Dude, and thus won't be responsible for the apocalypse.

OK, this is going to be hard to believe but me and Mike Stevens have just discovered some majestic shit. And I would NOT have come to this conclusion unless we researched it A LOT. Which we did. So now, I think I can tell you. Should I just say it?

Yeah, definitely.

It has come to my knowledge over the past couple minutes that I'm probably a MOTHERFUCKING EARL! (It's like a high-ranking person that gets special privileges because a queen says so.)

Exhibit J: Proof of Earldom

<u>Detail</u>: Item received at 1500 EST, regular postage . . .

But don't worry, amigos, *I'm still going to be the same guy*. Will I be a dick to people that I wasn't to before? Nay, I won't.

Most people would.

There are many who would do that, and I think it's disgusting. So relax. I'll just be able to legally make people chill with me if the situation requires or if I deem it so. And if I'm walking down the street and somebody is drinking pop and I see it, I can legally force them to give me a sip or give me something of equal or greater value, like three French fries.

We're all pretty pumped about it. There's going to be a big party at Todd "Semen" Niemen's house. Four people have already said they'd be my squire. Mike will definitely be the highest-ranking one. But I am thinking of having my second squire just be a temporary slot for a couple different people because their girlfriends wouldn't understand or their bosses are dicks.

None of us can believe it, but isn't that how this stuff happens? It just comes so quickly that we have no time to emotionally prepare ourselves.[28]

So now people will have to take us seriously. This is exactly the sort of thing that will give an air of respect-ability to us flipping out and whipping swords around. And there is no way a mayor would deny thee an audience if I send him a letter with a wax seal and shit.

I definitely feel like I've got way more power. Like all this stuff that's happening—it's like it's meant to be. We're supposed to find Derek Wood and open up this portal and battle interdimensional beings and save the world and get blow jobs from our soul mates. BUT, when our accomplishments bring us almost legendary status, we'll still be the same dudes *no matter what.* I'm not going to eat a single crumpet or write one play review.

---

[28] If all this stuff about the Legend and being an earl is true, then it totally confirms what I've been feeling since last year. That is, I've been chosen to do something for the advancement of mankind, and I'm pretty much way better than everybody I know.

Yeah, totally.

So the most important thing is that now, more than ever, we've got a mission. Let's get that portal open and find Derek—it's our damn destiny.

What about eating sushi? Are we going to start doing that?

Hell no, I don't eat sushi, bitch.

All right, sorry, man.

Shit.

The Earl Oath

On my honor, as an Earl, I promise to:

1. Not be a dick.

2. Duel anyone who challenges me.

3. Eat grapes out of the bosoms of concubines.

4. Master the crossbow and broadsword.

5. Cherish the Unicorn.

6. Stop staring at legless people.

That's pretty mature of you.

I know.

23:

Back to Work

IN THE MORNING I walk downstairs, and I ask my mom if I was a virgin birth. She says no. Slut.

Most people, after realizing that they are an earl, would take a vacation or lay in the backyard imagining the political power they wield. Not me. I call up Mike Stevens and we go to work right away. Trust me, I'm totally willing to enjoy the pomp and majesty of being an earl, but our current task of getting Derek back and fighting interdimensional beings in the Immortal Realm is more pressing.

Mike informs me that his cousin may have some information about Derek Wood's disappearance.

CLUES:

* The foam in toothpaste doesn't do anything.

* I'm probably an earl.

Yo, my cousin might know something.

OK, cool. So we drive over to Mike Stevens's cousin's house.
When we get there, Mike's cousin is like, "Yo." And we're
like, "Yo." Without wasting time, I ask him if he knows something about Derek's death, and he says, "No."

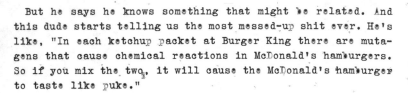

Fuck.

But he says he knows something that might be related. And
this dude starts telling us the most messed-up shit ever. He's
like, "In each ketchup packet at Burger King there are muta-
gens that cause chemical reactions in McDonald's hamburgers.
So if you mix the two, it will cause the McDonald's hamburger
to taste like puke."

It's true. I put sauce
from one place on the other place's burger.
After taking one bite, I threw it against the
wall and screamed in fury.

"Yeah, and McDonald's immediately responded by extending
an attack to THEIR Dipping Sauce Line and the Honey Mustard
Sauce to mutilate Burger King burgers.

"Then things spun out of control with each side having corporate scientists working vigorously to make their condiments
destroy the other side's burgers. Now there is a Burger War
going on where these companies are working on their burger
defenses to counteract the condiment's destructive properties
and render them safe against the sauces!"

Having now gotten more information than I dared to hope,
I move on to more general topics of Eric Koller boning Dawn
Baynard. Mike's cousin promptly confirms our suspicions about
her feeding him a pretzel and its logical conclusion.

We immediately leave and reflect with satisfaction on this
afternoon's progress. On our way home, we see Jeff Trenton
chasing Cindy Gold's dog.

JEFF TRENTON: A LIFE. CONTINUED

Recently it is becoming clear to us that Jeff Trenton's behavior is more erratic than we can handle. Shooting a bottle rocket from his O-ring, lying about the extra donuts, unjustified face punching over a Cabo Chicken Sub Sandwich. I understand that people have varying levels of eccentricity. All humans have their specific needs, and we spend our lives struggling to fulfill those needs. However, those needs need not be too exotic—some sleep, a tug job, a burrito. <u>But that's it</u>. There is something about the needs of Jeff Trenton that sets him apart from the everyman.

I saw him sniff Chris Forest's underwear yesterday. Plus he keeps trying to walk in on Shannon while she's peeing.

If he were just some dude in the neighborhood, Mike Stevens and I would have merely reserved ourselves to throwing sticks at him. But he is a member of our Elite Fighting Force of Dudes, and we cannot let him sabotage the mission. *He knows too much.*

Mike and I now conclude that there must have been a beginning to this behavior—a single day, where an event, not necessarily traumatic, caused him to change. Perhaps his mom tried to strangle him, or he was forced to shave his dad's back. Nobody knows. Whatever happened, the shift wasn't a conscious one but it was, perhaps, the end of a normal, integrated human being. There must have been one day in his life when Jeff Trenton, the well-adjusted boy, became Jeff Trenton—

—the textbook anal sadist.

One moment the guy would be sharing a taco with a dear friend, and the next moment, Jeff would be smothering that same friend with a plastic bag because they wouldn't let him stick a pencil up their butt.

I remember when I was younger, my dad would take me out for ice cream and a spanking, but you get over it.

Some don't. It could have been anything. Maybe his grandparents were nudists. We'll never know. Whatever that soapy, sudsy experience was, it has left him with the insatiable, infantile, substitute need to slap cats together.

If the mother abruptly stops breast-feeding, the baby will become a chain smoker. The mother's milk dries up.

From now on we have to watch him closely. Although he is a full member of our team, he could destroy us if he joins the Dark Side. Plus, if he goes, we'll only have three people left on the team.

PSYCHIC

THOUGHT

On August 17, 3029, something huge is going to happen. I don't know what exactly, but if any dude from the future reads this, just make sure to chill out that day.

W E D N E S D A Y

24:

More "Indian" Activity

THE "INDIAN" is planning something big. So far he hasn't come out of his habitat to retrieve usable calcium in over forty-eight hours. Yet this week the lawn is mysteriously mowed.

The increase in "Indian" activity forces us to implement every possible resource, even it means dealing with Pure Evil.

CLUES:

* There is a Burger War going on, and we may be right in the middle of it.

* Jeff Trenton is not to be trusted.

* Eric Koller and Dawn Baynard *made love.*

Yes, warlocks. I hate having to resort to this type of person for knowledge, but if it can get us any closer to the truth, it's worth it.

Reluctantly, Mike and I walk over to the house of Chris Barton, a known warlock and immortal, to gather information.

When we get there, Chris Barton is already at the window waiting for us, *like he knew we were coming.* Discreetly concealing any sign of interest, I casually ask him if he knows about any "Indian" nocturnal activities or Hot Pocket clues. He says he knows nothing. I study him carefully but can make nothing of the validity of his claims.

But he does tell us some theory about how every time you hear of a beached whale found closer and closer inland, they're training to live on land and take over.

And then, *after knowing us for only five minutes,* Chris Barton suddenly feels compelled, I do not know why, to start talking about his personal life, totally crossing over our emotional boundaries. He tells this dumb long story about how his dad kissed him on the lips once. And then, at the end of the story, the guy is like, "I feel really messed up right now. Could one of you give me a haircut?" We quickly recognize this as a clear attempt to use guilt as a tool. Mike and I are disgusted and immediately terminate the interview. We vow to never consult warlocks again.

Later, Mike Stevens and I go back to my house and plan for the next Elite Fighting Force meeting. No new members joined us to counter the "Indian" activity. The earl title does attract a few new people to the meetings. However, none are willing to sign the allegiance contract after they read the noncompete clause, which basically states we could kill them if they joined a similar group.

So far the main group members consist of:

Trey Hamburger, Mission Commander Class A

Mike Stevens, Mission Commander Class B

Jeff Trenton, Sabbatical/Dealing with Issues

Todd "Semen" Niemen, Sunday through Wednesday—Full Member; Thursday through Saturday—at his dad's house.

Derek Wood (Dead), Honorary Member

Supposedly, Ed Trimmel was going to provide assistance, although we never figured out what he was going to do.

I think if we had British accents people would take us A LOT more seriously.

Whatever happens with the group is a moot point. We must now begin the first stage of our departure to another dimension. Since Professor Timothyq Arnoldsq wasn't able to supply us with any information for opening a portal, we'll have to improvise. There may be a way to do it without any expensive equipment, and I'm pretty sure it has something to do with our brains.

25:

Linking Brains Together

OK, we only use about 12 percent of our brain, and the rest just sits there, chillin'. I believe that somehow, every one of us can unlock that other 88 percent.

Albert Einstein was the smartest man to ever live. It has been said that his brain capability was over 22 percent, and he also had a unique strength that nobody could explain. The only thing was that he ended up going nuts toward the end.

EINSTEIN, THE LATER YEARS

It's a risk that some are willing to take.[29]

Our goal is to increase the brain's potential. And we have discovered a way to do it. Me and Mike are going to link our brains together and mimic the information-gathering and scanning ability of a brain way smarter than ours. One problem is the signals from his brain and my brain must be combined precisely and then fed into something.

Intelligence is mainly a mixture of the application of common sense and good basic husbandry.

When the two brains are totally in sync they can create powerful beams of energy that can crumple space/time and then allow a couple of dudes to cross the space/time threshold if they really want to.

As for now, we don't have any appreciation for the type of shit we'll be able to achieve once we combine our brains together. We might start speaking in Chinese or solve thousand-year-old mysteries. Who knows, but it's worth a shot. Whatever happens, we're going to try for the last time to get some funding. We'll need it—big-time.

---

[29]**ALBERT EINSTEIN'S LIFE**
1879 Einstein is born. • **1902** He starts working at a Swiss Patent Office. Hates it. • **1903** In March, Einstein receives a mysterious package in the mail containing some weird-ass substance. • **1904** Einstein's boss tells him to get out of his face. Einstein gets angry and injects the substance. • **1905** Out of nowhere he starts inventing all these inventions *and nobody knows how.* • **1952** Einstein's strength increases. He crushes a coworker's head and immediately goes into hiding. • **1955** He's basically nuts at this point and busts up his living room. He dies later that night when his house ignites into a fiery inferno.

POSSIBLE NEW ABILITIES.
DON'T KNOW FOR SURE THOUGH

- speak with our minds
- move objects with only our thoughts
- help/control others
- solve complex equations
- become better persons/people

Imagine if we had food powers, and could zap food into our mouths.

OK, now seriously, this will be the last time I'll have to
address this. If Mike Stevens and I link our brains together,
I do not want him to suffer public humiliation for any of my
past transgressions. So Dawn Baynard, if you're reading this,
I have to clear something up with you as well. Do you remember
on Tuesday when you walked past my window and saw me sitting on the couch, BUCK NAKED, bouncing a meticulously folded
pillow on my lap? OK, you have to listen to me carefully. I
wasn't jerking off. Yes, I know, the probability of the same
man being falsely accused of jerking off on three separate
occasions in the same week is astronomical, but I'm sure once
you hear my explanation, you'll agree—*it's definitely possible.* What happened was, I just finished cooking some potato
poppers in the oven, and I was hot from the excess oven heat.
Hence, no clothes. So I sat on the couch, and I put a pillow
between me and the pan because the pan was hot too. And all
of a sudden one of the potato poppers fell out of my mouth
and tumbled down my stomach and fell into a never-before-seen
hole in the pillow. When you walked by my window, I was merely

trying to extract the potato popper from the pillow by banging
it rhythmically against my own midsection. So there it is.
There's no need to punish a man for having high standards of
pillow hygiene—something, I think, everyone could agree on.
I hope this puts things in perspective, and we can move on
in an orderly and mature fashion.

That's a totally reasonable explanation, and, frankly, it was unnecessary for you to even clarify what happened. People should just know you're not that kind of guy.

    Now, Dawn, I've known you for a while, and you should real-
ize that is something I would never do. So, after this, I hope
we never have to return to that day in our minds—

—or in our hearts.

    And, in good faith, Dawn, I would like to extend to you an
offer of friendship. I would just like to inform you that I'm
putting together a picture collage of all my friends, and in
a conciliatory effort, I would like to invite you to be part
of it. Pretty dorky, huh? So, if you got a minute, would you
mind sending me a picture of yourself? Any picture will do,
but if you have one where you're in a bathing suit, bending
over, that would be perfect. In the picture, your back WILL
BE ARCHED. And you will be wearing high heels. I also like
fishnet panty hose—black. And a top hat. That's the only way.
So . . . great! I think it would be a great addition to my

Collage of Friends. Right now, I'm cutting out construction
paper of varying colors for the border.

Otherwise the whole thing will be RUINED.

And please note that my collage will in no way be used for
masturbatory purposes because I don't do that.

Thanks. People are so cynical sometimes.

Trey Hamburger
681 Lake George Road
Leonard, MI 48367

March 12, 2008

Forest Conservation Society of America
attn: Awards, Fellowships & Grants Manager
Marie Y. Lander
P.O. Box 6190
Boulder, CO 80301-6190

Dear Forest Conservation Society of America Science Grant
Committee,

OK, listen up. Time is running out and I have some
important issues to talk about.

It so happens that we both have something the other guy
wants. You people have grant money. WE have discovered
something fundamentally awesome, and we definitely would like
to give you guys an opportunity to be a part of it. (Don't
worry, this is NOT your typical penis-enlargement scheme.)

First let's get the money part out of the way. We
estimate that we would need about 100 million dollars
each. All of the money will be used for research and
NOTHING ELSE. I'm sure you got a lot of people who would
go insane if they got ahold of that kind of dough. Rest
assured, we wouldn't.

I have invented many things and have never done a thing
about it, but that's about to change if we get that
money. For example, counterclockwise watches. Imagine how
many of those we could sell. But for this project, we'll
be working with things way more profound.

My associate and I plan on linking our brains together
to open a rift in space/time. And when we get to the
other side, *we will engage in combat*. But don't worry,
our work is based on the work of well-known scientists
(Einstein, Newton, Aristotle, etc.) and the work of lesser
well-known dudes we know personally. (Sorry I can't go
much more into this, but I think my neighbor, or someone
in my area, is working for the other side. We'll tell you
about that later once all the paperwork is finished.)

IF YOU WOULD LIKE TO MEET FOR TEA AND DISCUSS THIS
FURTHER, THEN THAT CAN DEFINITELY BE ARRANGED.

Right now, you probably have a lot of questions about
our research and how it might affect the people of Planet
Earth. BUT, we've got some questions for you too.

   i. Can we choose to receive the money monthly or in one
      huge sum, like the lottery?
  ii. Are you people biased against regular people in your
      grant decision-making? If so, do you think that's

even legal? (Todd "Semen" Niemen's uncle is a tax
attorney and is itching for a case like this . . .)
iii. Are you ready to take a chance on two dudes who
believe in their hearts that they can do some
messed-up shit in the laboratory like create a portal
to another dimension or maybe even, I don't know,
go wild with some solvents and start creating this
bio-slime that will change the way we fundamentally
think about the existence of shrimp and/or Hawaii?
iv. Oh, and if we end up not getting our project done,
do we have to give the money back?

Look, I know this stuff is outside of the established
academic milieu, but if only one person saw the truth,
and gave us this chance, we'd owe them big-time. (That
might be you.) Plus, I got a lot of payments and if I
could get this money, man, it would really help out.
That's all I'm going to say about that right now.

Au revoir,
Trey Hamburger, Lead Project Scientist and Mission
Commander Class A
Mike Stevens, Lab Assistant and Mission Commander Class B

P.S. Is it safe to eat only chicken nuggets for extended
periods of time?

REPLY FROM LADY

Forest Conservation Society of America
Awards, Fellowships & Grants Manager
Marie Y. Lander
P.O. Box 6190
Boulder, CO 80301-6190

Trey Hamburger
601 Lake George Road
Leonard, MT 48367

March 24, 2008

Mr. Hamburger,

Your application for the 2009 Science Grant was received
on March 14, 2008.

Thank you for your interest in our 2009 Science Grant. Our institution offers a $20,000; $35,000; and $50,000 grant. We do not offer a $100,000,000 grant. There have been many applications this year, and not all of them fulfill our requirements for endorsement. Your application is one of those. Although interesting, your research may be too avant-garde for our institution, and we have decided to pursue applicants who more closely reflect the requirements for our grant—namely, those relating to *forest conservation*. In effect, we will not be contacting you for an interview in the second phase of our grant process.

More specifically in response to your letter, we do recognize the enthusiasm of "regular people" engaging in scientific endeavor. However, the Forest Conservation Society of America Grant Foundation reserves the right to craft its own selection criteria that are consistent with federal and state discrimination laws. Because of that right, we do not have to participate in encouraging or developing scientific opinions that the Foundation may not share—counterclockwise watches or bio-slime, for that matter.

If you have any other questions regarding our selection process or the Forest Conservation Society of America Grant Foundation, we can be contacted at:

Forest Conservation Society of America
P.O. Box 6190
Boulder, CO 80301-6190
Or
grants@forestconservationsociety.org

Sincerely,
Marie Y. Lander

P.S. "Having a lot of payments to make" does not constitute a legitimate reason to be awarded a science grant.

Trey Hamburger
681 Lake George Road
Leonard, MI 48367

Forest Conservation Society of America
attn: Awards, Fellowships & Grants Manager
Marie Y. Lander
P.O. Box 6190
Boulder, CO 80301-6190

Dear Marie Y. Lander,

Would the fact that I am an Earl change anything?

Thanks,
Trey Hamburger

REPLY FROM LADY

Forest Conservation Society of America
Awards, Fellowships & Grants Manager
Marie Y. Lander
P.O. Box 6190
Boulder, CO 80301-6190

Trey Hamburger
681 Lake George Road
Leonard, MI 48367

April 3, 2008

No.

Marie Y. Lander.

It's possible that Mrs. Lander has a urinary tract infection. (It's basically a virus that slightly irritates the vaginal region, which may explain her negative attitude.)

Well that's no reason to deny a research grant.

I totally agree.

I hate that shit. Dealing with all that shit in general. When we first decided to embark on this mission to beat a ghost/alien's ass, I had no idea how much red tape and office politics we would encounter.

Bullshit, huh?

Yeah, BULLSHIT. At a time like this. At the dawn of the future! FUCK, I wanna punch something.

In Cambodia, you can throw a hand grenade at water buffaloes for _five_ _bucks._

That sounds perfect right about now.

VAGINA TIP

If you drink a frozen Coke while you have a urinary tract infection, your vagina will explode.

26:

Getting Freaked Out

CLUES:

* Beached whales may become walking whales if no one does anything.

* "Indian's" lawn keeps getting mowed, *but nobody is mowing it.*

* The Grant Foundations are working together so that we don't get any money.

* Chris Barton's dad kissed him on the lips.

OK, Mike, Jeff, and I are now on Alert Level 9. A VERY trusted source who went through the hybrid's garbage found a Nestle Crunch bar wrapper.

> *My uncle used to work at Nestle and one day he noticed that they were putting something strange into the Crunch bar batter. He got out of that place fast.*

Shit. Maybe one day, a couple weeks from now, some dude will bite into a Crunch bar and Dead Derek's toe will be in their mouth.

That damn "Indian" thinks of us as a FOOD BASE, doesn't he?

These entities are known for using glandular secretions to form people into a food pulp.

He probably considers us bags of food!

I'm not a bag of food!

ME NEITHER!

And check this out. At 3:00 a.m. EST, two hours after Todd "Semen" Niemen went through the "Indian's" trash, *Mike Stevens's grandpa dies.* Mike's mom says it was a coronary heart condition. But we hear from Brad Turner that the old guy was impaled by a pike. Whoever did it may be the same guy that got Derek Wood. So (1) we have to attack the people that did this. (Probably the "Indian.") And (2) we have to prepare for a possible counterattack from Mike's grandpa. Since he has now passed on into the Immortal Realm, he will have acquired more powers and will most likely start using them.

Dude, with the sudden increase in paranormal activity, we must be real close to discovering the truth.

Yeah, totally. In addition to the "Indian" preparing to attack us, Derek dying, Mike's grandpa getting impaled, the gurgle sounds, and basically everything else, we STILL have to worry about sabotage from our fellow Elite Fighting Force of Dudes members. Jeff Trenton's behavior has become even MORE curious lately. Basically all the sentences coming out of his mouth are thrown together <u>without any justification</u>. Just yesterday, he said something that I have kept quiet *until now.* While we were in my basement watching TV, he looked over at me and said the following:

Dude, listen to this. I was thinking yesterday, in Spanish and shit. And you know how in Spanish masculine words end with the letter "o" and feminine words end with the letter "a"? Then I was like, <u>that means "salsa" is a feminine word.</u> So I got to thinking. When guys get together and watch football or play poker, they usually eat chips and salsa. But listen to this, what if some scientists get together and make some salsa, but make it exactly like normal salsa, and call it "SALSO-The Real Man's Dip." I'm sure a lot more guys would eat it.

I purposely made no reply to this, and kept still. Jeff, having said it, continued to lie on the floor, and quietly chew on a dog toy.

I remember once when he unintentionally called me "Mommy." I pretended not to notice.

From now on, we must completely keep Jeff Trenton ignorant of our plans, and consider him an enemy. Mike is feeding him false

information about us going to Daytona Beach on Thursday instead
of going to another dimension. So far, he believes everything
we tell him. I just wonder if he even knows he's sick.

*One is not one's own
psychoanalyst.*

Damn.

This work is mentally demanding, not because of the intellectual challenge, but because of the constant readiness for
something to attack you. YOU'RE JUST NEVER ABLE TO RELAX. Plus,
at night, when I finally DO fall asleep, my mom keeps eating
peanuts out of a plastic bag downstairs and <u>it keeps waking
me up</u>. I yell at her to stop it, and she yells at me to shut
up. And I yell at her for yelling at me! These conditions have
made it difficult to be well-rested for battle. Regardless, I
will not let this prevent me from ambushing an "Indian."

*Did you know that late
afternoon and early evening are PRIME
TIMES for hot flashes?*

WELL I DO NOW!

*Ladies, if you're having a hot
flash, don't be afraid to remove yourself
from a social setting. It may be the much-needed
break your vagina will thank you for.*

In addition to that, we've been more aware of possible
sabotage attempts as we approach our launch date. There may
even be attempts at mind control. Or there may not be. Either
way, you must make sure that every thought you have is your
own. *You may not even be reading this sentence.*

Yo, I think World Wrestling Federation and all their ring fighting is a conspiracy to encourage people to turn to violence in order to solve their problems, instead of just talking it over.

You may be right. In fact, right now you might think you're thinking what you think, but you may not be thinking what you think you're thinking. It may be that you're actually thinking about something *totally different.*

There have been times in my life where I have forgotten very important events (my birth, etc.). And since then I have come to the conclusion that I have been <u>neurolized</u> (I.E. MY MEMORY HAS BEEN ERASED).

And think about this: you were eating dinner last night. That is just a memory. You were eating dinner three weeks ago—that's just a memory too. Now, we forget what we had for dinner 99 percent of the time. And that pretty much goes on for most of our lives. Now IF our identity is basically our memories, then *we might not even exist.*

It is extremely hard to believe that we actually live in reality sometimes. However, I think we should realize that this statement means nothing, and indeed is nothing unless some dude makes it something.

BUT if something resonates within the depths of your catacombs and sends electrophonic shivers over your skin, then you know it has the Resonance of Truth within it. Only then can you believe your own thoughts.

This whole thing is way bigger than I ever thought. Trey, if you disappear, I will burn my house down in retaliation.

Thanks, amigo. Mike, can you look deep within your catacombs and discern what will happen tomorrow?

OK, I'm getting an image. We're running out of your house all burnt up and partially hairless, but it looks awesome.

I feel that has the Resonance of Truth within it. Now, it is time to push the boundary of space/time.

PSYCHIC THOUGHT

Aries: A friend with plenty of go-get-'em spirit will attack a homeless man outside of a local bistro. Reminder: DECLINE INVITE TO BISTRO.

4.

SPACE / TIME

T H U R S D A Y

27:

Finalizing Conjectures

ALL RIGHT, Mike's grandpa has not attacked us yet. However, we are ready when he does.

If my grandpa floats by, touches my cheek, and says he loves me, I will strike.

CLUES:

* That damn
  "Indian" is
  eating people.

* Mike has been
  neurolized.

* Jeff Trenton is an
  enemy now.

We are able to gather together $30 for crossing the space/time barrier. It's a little below our expectations. Todd "Semen" Niemen said he could get us three bars of solid gold by 10:00 a.m. EST today. Didn't happen though.

At 10:30 a.m. EST, my bitch mom comes in and asks me who called, and I say

nobody. And then she asks me what I did with my birthday money.
She has no right to ask an Earl that. So I don't say shit.

Our plan is to leave the house by 7:00 p.m. EST tonight, and
get to another dimension by 7:15 or 7:20. We cancel all of our
appointments on Friday so we can recover from the voyage.

The tasks today are to finish our experiments on interdimensional teleportation, finalize our conjectures regarding the
fundamental structures of wormhole dynamics, and engage an
"Indian" in close combat.

And yes, some of our experiments are conducted under "lax"
conditions—there was some guy, we don't know who exactly, who
was just laying on the basement/lab floor for a couple hours
during a trial run—but that in NO WAY means our postulates
are invalid.

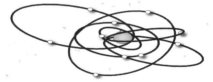

FUCKING ISOTOPES

After we finish the last of our experiments, Mike goes over
his pepperoni conjectures one last time, and then we try to
visualize the minutiae of the universe. We get nowhere.

The dude who invented fire must have been the craziest fuck ever. Imagine some guy just sitting there with some sticks, and then, all of sudden, he just starts rubbing them together? All them cavemen MUST have been like, "What the hell is this motherfucker doing?"

EXPERIMENTAL GUIDELINES

THE SCIENTIFIC METHOD

THE SCIENTIFIC METHOD CONT.

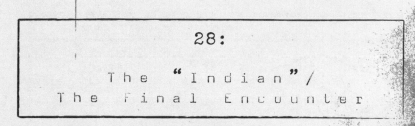

28:
The "Indian"/
The Final Encounter

NOW, before we transcend the limits of space/time, we have to finish one last thing here in the Mortal Realm.

The "*INDIAN*."

PSYCHIC
THOUGHT

OK, I'm getting a premonition that there is some dude out there who likes dudes. The dude reading this may be thinking, "Dude, I'm not that dude. I don't *like dudes."* *But that very dude would be wrong.* **He LOVES dudes.**

The deliberate efforts of this powerful being have not yet deterred us, but have made our mission more important. Regardless, we must hurry. Each day the gurgling noise is becoming even more violent. Whatever is out there is becoming more powerful.

Mike, have you ever thought about how close we are to knowing the answer to all this? From the Hot Pockets to the flipper mark to the secret government organizations and gurgles?

Well, by not Knowing anything in the first place, we don't have any idea how close to Knowing we are. Who Knows, we might be very close to Knowing, and may not even Know it!

What I do know is that this time the "Indian" won't be in diplomatic mode.

And his combat symbiotes will be FULLY EXTRUDED.

MISSION PREPARATION

Todd "Semen" Niemen and Mike Stevens meet at my house at 11:00 a.m. EST to plan for the Final Encounter.

We immediately spread out our equipment on the floor and begin going over diagrams of known amphibian pressure points. Mike Stevens and I pass out a pamphlet titled "Ghosts/Aliens" that contains all of the information gathered in the last week. Each Fighting Force member studies the pamphlet carefully.

After several hours of deliberation and careful analysis, we devise a plan to go in through the back door. Decoy dudes had been sent out earlier to conduct false insertions into the *front door* to confuse the "Indian."

Some dudes may even think this is a suicide mission.

Hopefully those dudes are wrong. Regardless, each Elite Fighting Force member makes a pact that if one of us gets injured or dehydrated, then another member must strangle the dehydrated guy to death so that the rest of the group isn't slowed down.

Cold calculations are not uncommon on operations like this.

Nearing our departure, we recheck our inventory one last time. Each man is loaded down with 140 pounds of shurikens, cleavers, baseball bats, chips and salso., claw hammers, and bow staffs. Every member has enough firepower to defend himself for several hours in case the other amigos are bogged down during the back door sweep. Any longer than that, *and the dude will die.*

For several days we practiced and trained for this moment. We had timed ourselves to see how long it would take to rip open a simulated head (watermelon).[30]

Dude, after we finish this we should organize a freelance mission to recover American POWs still trapped in Mexico.

It would be a waste of training if we didn't.

[30]Seven seconds.

We studied microterrain analyses, meteorological surveys, rules of engagement, zoological classifications, local politics, the chart of elements, beekeeping. Never before had so few dudes considered so many details.

I am willing to take the very same oath, minus the death part.

MISSION EXECUTION

As we approach the "Indian's" back window, no one speaks. Only hand signals are exchanged. I look over at Todd "Semen" Niemen. He is supposed to be keeping watch but he falls asleep. And NOW I find out that Ed Trimmel forgot the advanced avionics and countermeasure equipment. *At the greatest moment of my life, my amigos have bequeathed me.*

It doesn't matter though. This morning we sequestered ourselves in isolation and planned for everything that might go wrong. And the execution of this operation will be the fruit of all our hard work. The only way that our mission could be compromised is if something occurs that we hadn't planned for.

Which is exactly what happens.

We peer into the "Indian's" back window and—

The Indian is just a regular dude.

A very disgusting dude.

One of the most intense intelligence surveillance missions of our lives, and it was just some dude watching *Black Cock 4: White Man's Nightmare*.

This is not the terrifying climax I was hoping for.

At this very moment, our entire investigation is in turmoil.

Damn, I thought we were so close to discovering the truth about ghosts/aliens. Dude, could it be possible that the "Indian"/Indian may have been doing something totally unrelated to jerking off but that could very easily be misinterpreted as jerking off? I mean, maybe his tooth popped out and embedded itself into his jeans and he was merely trying to dislodge the tooth from the cloth by rhythmically tapping the fibers.

We must pursue the simplest explanation, and as scientists, we must always be vigilant to see things for what they are regardless of our aims. That damn Indian was jerking off. And there's no reason we should attribute to him any other explanation. You saw what he was doing, and it was disgusting.

You're right. We're scientists.

Afterward we dissect the mission in intricate detail, and analyze what went wrong. Only later would we privately agonize over the sacrifice we had been forced to make. But for now, we walk over to Walters Lake again, and with the wind blowing in our faces, we get pissed.

Damn.

Trey Hamburger
681 Lake George Road
Leonard, MI 48367

March 13, 2008

Pitambara Santhanam
Dept. of Physics
Winter Hall
Rochester University
Santa Barbara, CA 93106-9530

Dear Professor Pitambara Santhanam,

I investigated my neighbor more, and he's not a pure-blooded alien. He's merely Indian, and, due to legal reasons, I cannot discuss this situation further. (I hope this won't affect the possibility of us working together in the future.)

Sorry,
Trey Hamburger, scientist

P.S. If you know any colleagues that have been acting unusual lately, let me know *immediately*.

29:

Regroup

SOMETIMES an "Indian" is just an Indian. Anybody put in our position would have thought the same thing.

He was seen eating fries with a fucking fork. Who could have known?

And he blew through a yield sign like *he's never seen one before in his life.* We made the best decision we could with the information we had. We can't keep blaming ourselves.

C L U E S :

* The Indian jerks it.

* The Indian is a regular dude.

> *You throw a stick at ONE INDIAN and everybody thinks you're a DICK.*

It doesn't matter that the Indian dude was just a regular dude. How many times did Isaac Newton fail before he invented the Fig Newton?

> *Tons.*

This is our chance to leave our Mark on History. Just because we made one silly mistake of attacking a man while he's in the act of masturbation does NOT, in any way, mean we cannot cross the space/time barrier.

> *Did you know that for all of Isaac Newton's remarkable inventions, he never saw a buck-naked lady?*

I can believe that.

Pitambara Santhanam
Dept. of Physics
Winter Hall
Rochester University
Santa Barbara, CA 93106-9530
March 31, 2008

Dear Mr. Trey Hamburger,

I am happy to hear that your neighbor is not from another planet. Being from India myself, I hope that your neighbor did not receive any harm because he was different.
    None of my colleagues has been acting strangely lately.

Salutations,
Pitambara Santhanam
Physics Department

30:

Opening the Portal

6:30 p.m. EST

All right, motherfuckers, the experiments are finalized and, after this afternoon's fuck-up, we have rebounded emotionally. We are now ready to begin the Dimensional Transference. The only thing left to do is prepare ourselves for something this intense. Derek Wood is still out there floating around in another dimension, chasing bubbles around, and <u>we are going to get him BACK</u>.

ALL RIGHT MOTHERFUCKER, LET'S DO THIS SHIT!

DISCLAIMER:

Crossing the space/time barrier should only be done by those of Pure Heart, and in no way should be used to do stuff other than whatever Mike Stevens and I ultimately decide to do. If you have lower-back problems, you should avoid this type of shit as well.

PREPARING YOUR MIND FOR TRANSPOSITION AND RESPECTING EMOTIONAL BOUNDARIES

IMPORTANT

The following are the conditions for making love to an alien, *if it comes up.*

* normal ass
* normal vagina
* be cool about it

I've heard of actual cases where experienced kung fu masters have frozen in transdimensional situations due to a lack of mental training. *The consequences of getting this one wrong could be HUGE.*

My old martial arts teacher was dating one of the students there. When she broke up with him, he karate-chopped her up pretty bad.

So the first thing we have to do is imagine going to a place where nobody speaks English. And I mean nobody. When I went to Mexico when I was thirteen, I couldn't even buy a Coke.

That's why I don't go anywhere!

Yeah, I know. It's just something we'll have to work through.

Second, be confident. While opening a portal you may experience doubts about whether you should even be doing this. You may even think this is ridiculous. *That's normal.*

And, during this process, if you start thinking about dicks other than your own <u>for whatever reason</u>, you may be gay. So watch out.

Some thoughts shouldn't even be thunk.

The third thing is not to freak out. Various emotions will be felt. Ignore them. Stay calm. Just keep moving. Saying anything negative may result in a galactic war, and I'm deadly serious. In case you start wiggin' out, soothe your mind by picturing yourself nude, riding a horse through a field while shooting a shotgun in the air.

I can't stop relaxing right now.

Good. Fourthly, you have to stay alert. It will look pretty cool at first, even disarmingly beautiful, but have no doubts that an alien could bust out of a plasma membrane and headbutt you without warning.

And lastly, expect Psychic Attacks.

Ladies, a psychic attack may leave you with tender breasts and possibly the Whoops Surprise Period! Though most people will never need to deal with this, some can't avoid it. Don't worry if it seems like you're having a heavier flow in the beginning of a surprise period, that's OK. _Most of the time it tapers off._

I'm sure this sounds dumb to some people out there, but I'm sure it makes total sense to others. While floating around, you may find yourself assaulted by dudes unknown. It's bullshit, I know. But there are beings out there who are going to start shit no matter what, and there's nothing you can do about it.

You're only responsible for your own actions.

However if you do get into a psychic battle, make sure to have your amigos there if you start losing.

I've been mind-raped twice. It's a touchy subject to talk about because of a whole lot of mental issues. The first time it happened, I was just sitting on the porch, and my OWN HAND started reaching for a glass of pop and _I wasn't thirsty at all._ But it kept moving closer even though I didn't want any pop. My hand brought the glass up to my mouth for a drink and I pressed my lips shut. Sweat droplets rolled down my forehead. When I realized it wouldn't end, I gave in and took a sip. After it happened, I immediately ran upstairs, laid in bed, and cried for the rest of the afternoon.

Three days later, when I found myself weeping over a fucking Faygo commercial on TV, I realized I couldn't battle this on my own. That's when I told my mom. She told me to shut up about it.

To this day, I don't know why I was chosen as a target, but I do know that whoever perpetrates these types of things is usually jealous of your social standing—women are drawn to me. In the meantime, I'm coping.

What happened the *second time* you were mind-raped?

> It is too horrible to mention, and by merely thinking about it I risk becoming unglued. All I can say is that it involved an entire tube of Preparation H and a corn dog.

Let us never speak of this again.

C O P I N G

In your mind, picture somebody you trust, somebody you can always count on. Now, whatever you do, DON'T imagine that person being mauled by a bear. Doing so would dramatically weaken your sense of security.

Trey Hamburger
681 Lake George Road
Leonard, MI 48367

March 13, 2008

Professor Edward McBride
Cliff View University
Physics Department
1220 University Lane
San Diego, CA 92107

Dear Professor Edward McBride,

Me and Mike Stevens are prepared to offer you a bad-ass opportunity. We have discovered a way to travel to another dimension.

We are traveling through space/time like today, and we need somebody to go with us, bad. If you're in, you're in. If not, well you can go back to staring out the window wondering if anyone is ever going to know the Real You.

Don't worry. We got the whole thing planned out. My job is to get everybody organized and pumped up about going. Mike Stevens's job is to be there emotionally and dietarily with different types of food sources. Your job would be to keep coordinates, help us navigate through space/time, and clean.

Let me go over some things first before you say *yes or no.*

Item 1: I noticed that you don't have any kids. That's good because we can't guarantee your safety. Although, if you get into trouble on the other side, Mike Stevens and I will back you up and we fully expect you to do the same. If this is a problem, please let us know immediately.

Item 2: You're going to have to bring your own weapons because we might not have any extra ones. Most likely we will, but you never know.

Item 3: If any of your colleagues have skills (archery, stealth, etc.) that would compliment the group's talents and they wouldn't be a dick on the trip, then definitely let them know too.

Item 4: Very important. You can't tell anybody else about this *unless you think they'd understand.*

Others have shirked at such an undertaking. Me and Mike Stevens are pretty loose about it. Although, we do know full well that we might die going through the portal, or even end up coming back hairless. Could you handle that? That's for you to decide. (By the way, if you ever decide to use Nair, READ THE DIRECTIONS.)

Yours truly,
Trey Hamburger and Mike Stevens, copilots/amigos

P.S. If you're NOT coming, then, who knows, maybe you'll spend an entire evening screaming in the bathtub when you realize what you're missing.

CLIFF VIEW UNIVERSITY
1220 University Lane, San Diego, CA 92107

Trey Hamburger
681 Lake George Road
Leonard, MI 48367

Dr. Edward McBride will be out of the office until
May 19, 2008. When Dr. McBride returns, he will resume his
position as associate professor. If this is an emergency
you can contact the physics department secretary, Jessica
Ortega, at 619-████████ or e-mail jortega@physics
cliffview.edu, and she can direct you accordingly.

Jessica Ortega
Department Secretary
Physics Department
Cliff View University

Physics Department Phone Number: 619-████████
Physics Department Fax Number: 619-████████

Every scientist reading this has the power to change, but
they choose to be dicks.

Can we ever break out of
this cycle?

Sometimes I wonder whether anybody gives a crap about anything.

Dude, don't be like that. We got to keep going.

Dude, should we just give up? This whole quest is like being in a gang. You fight and fight, and shoot guns all over town, but you don't even know why. And by the time you realize that, *it's too late*.

DUDE, did you hear about the guy in Canada whose feet were like little rabbit feet? He wanted to get some prosthetic feet, but his insurance wouldn't pay for it. Do you think he gave up and wore little boots for the rest of his life? NO WAY! He started charging people to rub his feet for good luck, and ended up making a shitload of money. And GUESS WHAT, when he could afford to get the operation, he didn't. He wanted rabbit hands!

Dude, what does that have to do with our quest?

OK, let me put it this way. Remember when we really wanted tacos and we couldn't find them anywhere in the fridge? What happened?

We kept looking.

We found them.

I guess that's how the Pope feels sometimes.

31:

In Case We
Don't Come Back

FIRST AND LAST WILL
OF
MR. TREY HAMBURGER

I, Mr. Trey Hamburger, a resident of Leonard, Michigan, being
of sound mind and memory do hereby make, publish, and declare
this to be my First and Last Will and Testimony, hereby
revoking all the shit I said on previous dates to previous
amigos.

ARTICLE 1
PERSONAL REPRESENTATION

I hereby name, constitute, and appoint Mr. Todd "Semen" Niemen to administer my estate of porn. Both Mr. Mike Stevens
and I have deposited our porn collection in Mr. Todd "Semen"
Niemen's basement so our moms don't go buck wild if they find
it after we're gone. In the event of our evaporations, anyone
who wasn't a dick to us during our lifetimes may feel free to
peruse the collection. I won't dwell on the awkward details
about how the porn will be divided up among you. Mr. Todd
"Semen" Niemen will administer that as he sees fit.

ARTICLE 2
BURIAL/PAYMENT OF DEBTS

After being in another dimension, should my body fail to
decompose, stuff it with firecrackers and blow it up on Tanya
Winter's lawn. (She threw an orange at me a couple months
ago.)

If I am ionized, then the rest of my money will go to Mr.
Mike Stevens if he survives for the purpose of completing
the mission. Everything can be divided as fit _as long as Jeff
Swibner in no way benefits from my demise._

As Earl, I have selected and trained a designated successor
in the event I get my ass beat and can't perform my duties.
So in such a case, I deem Mr. Mike Stevens to be my successor and to have all the powers and duties of being an Earl
bestowed upon him in case of my passing. Also, I bequeath my
last paycheck to Mr. Stevens if he survives. _And I expect
likewise, if he evaporates and I survive._

ARTICLE 3
CONFESSIONS

Below I have included a list of my confessions:

- A couple months ago, I threw a rock at my neighbor and she had to get stitches.
- I absolutely hate you Cindy. Especially your giant nose.
- Sometimes, if I'm in a hurry, I don't even wipe my own butt.
- My mom asked me to stir a pot full of mashed potatoes one time and I got mad and used my hand.

I make these statements while in full control of my faculties and rationality. Please understand that if we are ionized, we expected it, and there is no one else to blame.

Thank you,

Main guy: Trey Hamburger

Trey Hamburger

Witness/Amigo: Mike Stevens

MIKE STEVENS

32:

Crossing the
Space/Time Threshold

AT the heart of this portal is a place where space/time stops and all the laws of physics break down, a place so remote that the chicks there might not even shave their beavers. And it is there where we will find the answer to all the gurgles and the floating Hot Pockets, and hopefully find Derek Wood.

We may go to the inner depths of time, or just wind up in Kentucky. At the very least we hope that our persons will be respected under the maritime and space law treaties.

Mike and I recheck our supplies one last time, and *head for the kitchen.*

And then, right before Mike and I are about to transcend the depths of infinity, my fucking bitch mom comes in after running errands and asks if I want to *smell her armpits*, which

I HAVEN'T DONE IN OVER SIX MONTHS. I yell at her to get out
of here. Which she does immediately.

Because of the present lab conditions, we decide to post-
pone the protocol. Mike gets depressed, and I have an anxiety
attack—so we spend the rest of the afternoon punching trees
in the backyard.

DEALING WITH ANXIETY ATTACKS

1. Avoid caffeine.

2. Cut carbs.

3. Avoid high-fructose corn syrup.

4. Travel.

Your mother's vagina is going
through a lot right now. With the onset
of menopause, much of the greatly needed
sap production has dissipated in the fallopian
causeways, which has produced an irritable
temperament. So don't take it personally.

You're right. But still, it was an abusive comment. Although
I understand the cause of her behavior, I, in no way, con-
done it.

Perhaps that's all one could
hope for.

VAGINA TIP

Did you know that women going through menopause have a 30 percent higher susceptibility to gum disease?

Gum disease is serious shit.

Ladies, if you're going through menopause, hold your brush at a 45-degree angle so you can clean along the gum line.

FRIDAY

33:

OK, Really Crossing the Space/Time Threshold

MIKE Stevens and I wake up the next morning early. Regardless of what happens, whether someone is a dick to us or not, we will not stop from crossing the space/time barrier and discovering the truth.

Mike, what are our chances of succeeding?

.it repeating of course.
(Estimates of survival are based on the Leroy Jenkins equations.)

That's better than we usually get. As long as I'm the Chosen Dude in the prophecy/legend, everything should run smoothly.

PSYCHIC THOUGHT

Gemini: Next Tuesday night, your neighbor will be making herself chicken salad for dinner. That bowl of chicken salad, having been poorly positioned on the counter, will tip onto the floor, and your neighbor will slip on the fallen contents. If you position yourself near the back deck of her house—ground level—you will be able to clearly see her vagina as she is sprawled on the floor.

Trey Hamburger
681 Lake George Road
Leonard, MI 48367

March 14, 2008

Law Offices of Green and Montgomery
2015 West Grand Boulevard, Suite 1200
Detroit, MI 48202

Dear Law Offices of Green and Montgomery,

My associate Mike Stevens and I linked our brains together at 7:28 a.m. EST this morning, and we screwed up BIG TIME. However, it must be known that we didn't enter into this lightly. We knew we were risking possibly transposing our personalities, or even morphing into pastries. Regardless, we proceeded. Our goal was to enter into another dimension. Before we said the specific Latin Phrases and turned on the microwave, I asked Mike if he really wanted to do this, and *he said yeah*. So I'm pretty much clear legally, right? Mike pushed the defrost for poultry button. (This setting was recommended to us by some guy on the Internet who said he wasn't human.) And then it happened. I heard that you can violate the laws of physics if you do it briefly, but I never thought it would go this far. For at least ten minutes Mike and I *did not exist*. We were . . . someplace else. We were shown images of dogs and naked women. I've never been inside of a vestibule, but it reminded me of that kind of thing. That's the only way I can explain it. So we stayed there for what seemed like ten to fifteen minutes. We were not comfortable AT ALL. It's like that feeling you get when you use a handicapped bathroom. There's this vague sense that you shouldn't be there. So we just left.
    The good thing is that I'm still Trey and Mike is still Mike. The bad thing is that Mike has a huge burnt spot on his head now, and his mom is going to flip when she sees it. (Yeah, she sucks, I know.) So my legal questions are

(1) Do you know if Mike Stevens's mom has any legal rights to sue me?
and

(2) Can the Village of Leonard sue me if something else came back with us through the portal?
and

(3) Are you willing to represent me pro bono if (1) and/or (2) happens. On a side note, I have sent in an application for a research grant for a lot of money. So if you back me up now, you will make millions when we hit it big.

    We need your reply bad.

Thank you,
Trey Hamburger

Green and Montgomery, Divorce and Family Law
2015 West Grand Boulevard, Suite 1200
Detroit, MI 48202

Tel: 313-891-4000
Fax: 313-891-4008

Trey Hamburger
681 Lake George Road
Leonard, MI 48367

April 3, 2008

Trey Hamburger:

The Law Offices of Green and Montgomery are pleased that
you have expressed an interest in our law firm. However,
our staff has neither the time nor the legal background
in personal injury to help you in this case. Our focus is
geared more toward divorce law. We are happy to recommend
someone who is more familiar with personal injury
lawsuits, if you are willing to pay for the services.

Thank you for your interest,
Jean Miller
The Law Offices of Green and Montgomery

5.

WEIRD-ASS

REVELATIONS

S A T U R D A Y

34:

The Morning After

OK, I might not be the Chosen Dude, because I'm
pretty sure we just started the APOCALYPSE.

I don't want to sound alarmist, but I think we're all going
to fucking die. 'Tis a fool I am! What sin have thee com-
mitted? I have tried to understand shit that should not be
understood!

After we complete the dimensional transposition, somebody
calls my phone. There is screaming in the background and the
reception is all fuzzy. Then Ed Trimmel, speaking in a Scot-
tish accent, says, "Dude. Did you guys just open a portal?"

I hesitate for a moment and ask, "Why?"

And he's like, "Well, Number One, there's FUCKING FOG EVERY-
WHERE. And Number Two, I had some bird chase me up I-75 for
one hundred miles until my car ran out of gas."

We forgot to cleanse the
kitchen after the ceremony.

And unearthly things came through. I don't say anything to
Ed Trimmel and hang up the phone.

It's starting.

Later Mike and I hear reports all over the place that things
are talking that shouldn't be talking, like goats and ducks
and stuff. Psychic attacks have increased too.

Then, out of nowhere, the gurgle sound gurgles harder than
it has ever gurgled.

Right now, there is an e-mail circulating that the end of
the world is supposed to happen next Tuesday. And with our
transdimensional screwup, it may be right.

I can't find it but it was on the news on Univision (Mexican
news[31]). They said that the apocalypse will probably be any
time now. Plus, recently, everybody at my neighbor's church
has been filling plastic containers FULL of cookies and pie to
survive the end times.

I don't know, but the creepiest thing was that a baby was
born this morning, with a full head of hair, and teeth.

[31]Todd "Semen" Niemen knows Spanish.

And we got flowers popping up at the North Pole!

Something very big is happening—and the Earth is definitely pissed off. The end of human civilization on this Earth is near.

At any moment we may be unexpectedly showered with fresh fruit and vegetables.

Right now, Mike and I are in such a state of anxiety, we can't even sleep without passing out. OK, listen. Whatever this is, it's something way bigger than just us. How we deal with this type of thing defines us as a culture.

Poop nuggets are rolling down my leg.

And what we do next may have lasting effects on dudes we don't even know.

Peter Brenton, resident of 33124 Green Tree Lane, Scottsville, Tennessee, I don't even know you, but, dude, sorry.

MIKE, CHILL OUT FOR A FUCKING SECOND! This is a very important and interesting historical moment to be living through. We must make our next move carefully. Because, who knows, we may be very close to destroying any future opportunity of putting it in a woman's butt _for good._

Maybe we made the mistake of thinking that our basic problem was the texture of our existence, and that, in reality, traversing space/time would not solve any of our problems AT ALL.

That may be. But we may have some last options. Brad Turner mentioned once that _if you go to the meatball factory and sit in the water outside, you'll evaporate into the atmosphere._ This may be our final recourse if things get too bad. I don't know if we could do it. But I DO KNOW we got to stop this apocalypse.

Regardless of what happens, I really plan on getting my life in order this weekend.

35:

Nearly Exact
Predictions

WE stare out the window for a couple hours, waiting for the apocalypse. Mike Stevens sees some dude walking
by my house. The guy stops for a second and looks inside his
backpack. And that's when Mike throws a stick at him. The guy
immediately runs. <u>Plot foiled</u>. All morning Mike and I think
about how we could have prevented all of this. Maybe we should
have read the prophecy directions more closely. Or maybe we
should have gotten PhDs before opening an interdimensional
portal. Regardless, we accept that no one is going to help
out, and we have to deal with this on our own.

*My uncle has something in
my basement that he's been working on for
nearly twenty years. It should hold them back
for a while.*

Yes, but that's not a permanent solution.

I spend the whole afternoon crunching numbers and computing data that I've collected over the past few days. I won't write down the whole equation to it because it is too long, but what I basically did was combine all the dates with different letters and used logic and historical events to find the answer.

BASIC EQUATION

(Number of teleporting pastry sightings per week: 1 Hot Pocket)
Multiplied by
(Percentage of people who have heard a weird-ass gurgle per 10,000: 8.1 percent)
Plus
([Number of people who have choked on grapes and died] Divided by [Number of people who have choked on grapes and lived to tell the tale] .7448 People)
Plus
(Number of grandpas impaled by a pike within the last week: 1 grandpa)
Multiplied by
(Warlock sightings per year: 2 warlocks)
Plus
(Number of amigo evaporations per 10 amigos: .1 amigo)
Multiplied by
(Number of burgers obliterated by corporate espionage per 10,000 burgers: 65 burgers)
Multiplied by
(Midget to dwarf ratio: 1.2777 repeating)
Divided by

THE NUMBER OF DUDES WHO COULD STOP IT: TWO.

HELL YEAH!

After calculation, I strongly believe the correct date for the apocalypse is: 15434023496.2031 Q.

FUCK.

PREPARING FOR THE APOCALYPSE
(IN CASE WE DON'T STOP IT)

What to Do

If we do have a little time to live, we must spend that time responsibly. What would you do if you found out the world was going to end in twenty-four hours?

I would spend the first couple hours with my family and loved ones, and try to make up for as much lost time as I can. Then I would do everything I ever wanted to do. I'd go find my crush and attempt to have a conversation that actually goes beyond "Hello." I would go to her house, tell her that I love her, and then squeeze her titties and run. After that, I would proceed to kill all my enemies.

Look, dude, I would want to stand out front of my neighbor's house with my pants around my ankles and piss, but we have to think about this more realistically.

OK, how about this. I'd lift weights one last time. And then find a space shuttle, break into it, load dozens of people who are cool into the hull, and pack in as much canned foods as possible. Then have a crazy guy at the bottom of the shuttle with a lighter release the fuel and we'll fly off into the sunset.

Better. But if we can't find the space shuttle, then what? If this shit really goes down, we need to amass a bunch of weapons or start making some. We would have to organize several amigos to set up road ambushes and jump out on people leaving the city. We would have to work on realistic short-term goals for survival: (1) hone quick-minded defense skills (need to work on this <u>today</u>) and (2) get more boat experience so we can easily maneuver in oceans, canals, and rivers! And that's just a start.

That's good too, but we got to do more.

36:

Closing the Portal

MIKE AND I realize that surviving the apocalypse is probably way too much work.

> And we don't feel like hiding out in the forests of Madagascar for the rest of our lives.

PSYCHIC THOUGHT

Libra: You will accomplish more work than ever on Wednesday, all with the help of Positive Thinking. On Thursday, however, you'll spend the entire day on the toilet. Plan accordingly.

So we choose to stop it. Now, this will only be the second time in history that two guys would be wholly responsible for starting the apocalypse and then stopping it in *the same week*.

Can we replicate the exact conditions when we opened the portal? Maybe. However, we don't know exactly what those conditions were! Mike was eating chicken nuggets right when it happened. Is it likely that the nuggets had anything to do with it? Probably not. Can we be

totally sure? <u>No way</u>. Plus, Todd "Semen" Niemen says he's
not going to come back to my house to say the Latin phrases
unless we pay him $20. And there's no way we're paying him
that. But it would be madness to stop now.

Dude, I just noticed something. I think the dimensional transposition must have altered or rearranged the material substructure of my brain. Basically, I think I'm smarter than I was yesterday. Like I've been thinking. How did breast-feeding ever come to be? Did some baby just see a titty and then start sucking on it, and then spread the word?

Mike, that is probably the most probing question you've ever
posed. I can't even begin to answer it.[32]

Now, we have to go back to the beginning and figure out the
one thing that set these events in motion.

The Hot Pocket.

Everything that has happened in the last week started with that
damn Hot Pocket. In the beginning was the Hot Pocket, and the
Hot Pocket was with Derek, and the Hot Pocket slain Derek. And
it is through the Hot Pocket, we will stop the apocalypse.

Do you ever wonder whether this story about Hot Pockets is really a story about us? I mean, could this ultimately be a self-referential system that eludes/precludes reality?

I don't know. But we have to close the portal even if it
means fighting a conscious pastry.[33]

---

[32] I realize now that Mike Stevens's intelligence has surpassed mine. Whether this is
a good thing has yet to be decided. For now, I will have to watch him more carefully.
If he turns against me, I must be willing to scissor-kick him in the face.
[33] I may have to scissor-kick Mike sooner than I thought.

Dude, nobody else has done what we did. Other than my friend's uncle, who else do you know that has gone to another dimension and tried to engage in close combat with the people who live there?

No one.

And who else has experienced what we have, and came to all of those damning conclusions?

Nobody.

Dude, do you know what this means?

Trey Hamburger
681 Lake George Road
Leonard, MI 48367

March 15, 2008

Nobel Prize Committee
The Nobel Institute
Boks 8072 Blindern
N-0288 Oslo
Norway

Dear Nobel Prize Committee,

Nobel Prizes, who doesn't want one?
I would like to nominate myself and Mike Stevens for this year's Nobel Prize for Physics, or whatever category might fit our achievements. You might be asking yourself who is Trey Hamburger and Mike Stevens. Good question. We're a couple of simple people who were just screwing around with a microwave one night, postulating about

some far-out shit, and ended up developing some of the
Greatest Theories Known to Man. Plus we opened up a
portal to *another dimension*.

I have to admit, the thought of being up at the
podium, accepting the award, speaking to thousands of my
contemporaries and having them wish they were me is pretty
stirring. But that's NOT why we nominated ourselves.
We did it because there are a lot of people out there
who don't believe us about our work—for example, Chris
"Semen" Niemen (Todd "Semen" Niemen's cousin).

After we get our reward (hopefully), I'll have my
own lab and assistants. We'll be measuring and mixing
chemicals, whatever WE want to do. Then every once in a
while we'll have a day where we just sit around talking
about life and stuff. And during the weekends, I'll go
out to dinner and flabbergast my colleagues and friends
with my discoveries and salty language. Then later, when
I'm really old, I'll spend most of my free time painting
flattering pictures of myself and wearing vaguely Asian
clothing. And one day I'll *just disappear*. There will be
some news article with the title: "Sailor Vanishes at
Sea—Renowned Scientist/Wild Man." And that will be that.

OK, now let's get down to business. Are there any
conditions about how me and Mike spend the money if we get
it? I'm not asking because I would go nuts with the money.
It's just that Ed Trimmel keeps asking me, and I don't
know what to say.

OK, look, if I don't get this award, I'll probably end up
working at the meatball factory like everyone else in town.

Trey Hamburger, Scientist/Mission Commander

P.S. I don't want to rely on this, but if it would
help . . . I'm an Earl.

Dude, the meatball factory
closed two years ago.

I know, but when they read that they'll be so emotional they
won't be able to say no.

Yeah, they'd have to be
heartless to resist.

37:

P r o v i n g   I t   A l l

I don't know whether or not we will get the Nobel
Prize. But, if we die trying to close the portal, let these
words be read at my coronation ceremony.

Dear Scientists of Planet Earth,

I, Trey Hamburger, am prepared to state that I have been
to locations unknown and had interfacing with various beings.
Here is my deposition.

DECLARATION OF TREY HAMBURGER

I, Trey Hamburger, declare as follows:

I have personal knowledge of the facts stated herein. I've
heard noises, smelled things I couldn't possibly have smelled.
Certain pastries have been observed in a manner suggestive of
extraterrestrial origin. I have uncovered conspiracies about
intense burger wars and the importance of toothpaste foam. I
have even interfaced with an Indian.

The following are conclusions based on those experiences.
Take from it what you will . . .

1. I have found that after hearing about or experiencing
    some weird shit, often, no matter how stupid it sounds
    or how much I didn't want to believe it was true, it
    ended up being true, despite evidence to the contrary.

2. I believe there is incontrovertible proof of a snack-
   food conspiracy, possibly rising to the highest levels
   of World Government.
3. An immortal will never tell you their true age. (That's
   how they live so damn long.)
4. It's very important, as scientists, that we don't
   dismiss ideas because they're retarded. When we ask
   about the nature of reality, don't you think, deep down
   in your heart of hearts, that the answer actually IS
   retarded? Any answer that ISN'T retarded would probably
   be a huge letdown.
5. Once you learn to cherish yourself, life becomes A LOT
   easier.
6. I understand that there is an assumption in science that
   the most elegant theory—the theory that postulates the
   fewest metaphysical entities and teleporting pastries—
   is the preferred theory. But what if you saw some dude
   float? *There's no way you could just scoff at that.*
7. And finally, I, Trey Hamburger would never eat dick-
   shaped crackers.

These are the mature fruits of a reasonable dude. I threw
myself into my work. I studied telekinesis as well as laser
technology and broadsword techniques. I was even willing to
befriend a hillbilly. My colleagues and I created an Elite
Fighting Force. Even by Special Operations standards we were
overtrained. My team members and I have spied on ducks and
Indians. Success is still elusive though. So far, all attempts
at reaching any understanding of infinity have been futile. And
I have suffered greatly for my cosmopolitan convictions.

Fortunately, our findings, though simple, have some bad-ass
implications. Theories that explain some long-standing scientific puzzles, like how to open dimensional portals, and how
one dude can know what another dude is thinking without that
dude *saying a word.*

In the end though, this may just be a story about some dudes
who tried to figure out some shit. It didn't work out and they
got pissed, and sometimes that's what happens. The only thing
that matters is that we Earls have to remember that we have no
natural enemy, only ourselves as the enemy we must overcome,
and DUDE WHAT THE FUCK! OK, I just found out something HUGE.
I'm not really an Earl. I just read a piece of mail wrong.
Man, FUCK EVERYBODY.

EXHIBIT K: PROOF OF EARLDOM REVISITED

10X MAGNIFICATION

38:

F u c k

Dude, I can't believe you're not an Earl...

FUCK. Mike and I both have anxiety attacks, but we recover almost immediately. Apparently the mailman screwed up big time.

He does not deserve the title he holds.

And now a lot of people think that Brent Spencer is the ACTUAL Chosen Dude!

But Brent Spencer is a DICK!

I KNOW! It's bullshit.

I don't give a fuck. I'll still be your squire.

Thanks, man. If it was four hundred years ago, I would definitely give you some land for saying that shit. But dude, there's no way somebody is going to take us seriously. Man, what the hell are we going to do now? What's the meaning of our lives?

39:

Meaning of Life

I'LL be quite frank about the absurdity of man's condition. We're fucked. Think about the first dude who became aware of himself. Man, that dude must have been WEIRD. Just imagine you're back in the Dinosaurs Times, and you're just walking around and the only thing you got to worry about is picking berries. And then BOOM you're thinking, *Damn, what's the point.*

AND THEN you'd go back to the huts, and everybody would be chowing down, and you'd be like, "Dude, why do we have to do anything?" And everybody would just be looking at you like, *Motherfucker, where are those goddamn berries!*

Nobody would understand what you're going through.

If I were that dude, I would start ripping up other people's tepees and start throwing sticks at the other tribespeople.

I'd like to say that I'd be above that type of behavior, but I can't. I would probably throw sticks at the tribespeople too.

Most of us think that when we die we'll get the answer to the meaning of life. But what if when we get there, everybody is standing around not doing shit, and you walk over to some guy and ask what's going on, and he is like, "I don't know, I was going to ask you."

Well, that seventy-six virgin thing is quasi true.

Well yeah. But still, we don't know the rest of it. Even Aristotle *said* he knew the meaning of life.

If Aristotle was so smart, how come he's dead?

Exactly. But the truth is that we haven't made any progress since that first conscious dude. Yeah, we got penicillin and pocket pussies. But at the end of the day, we're just making a bunch of stuff and we're no closer to an answer.

We don't even understand what a meow means!

I KNOW. WHAT THE FUCK ARE WE GOING TO DO! How can we begin to understand the minutiae of the universe when we can't even get a woman to let us put it in her butt! And with Derek being dead, everything seems different. I thought that only grandpas died. And so as long as I never have kids or adopt anyone with kids, I would be fine. But now, *any one of us could die.*

Who was it that first said that life should have meaning?

Barbra Streisand.

And why are we supposed to listen to her!

I don't know!

Man, being conscious is retarded.

    Like, I think that people get an impression of what the
meaning of life is supposed to be from movies or TV. That's
the stuff we watch when we want to get away from the world.
The world is some guy eating Hot Pockets for thirty years.
It's slipping in the shower and dying, or choking on a chi-
michanga. Who would go watch a movie where the main guy dies
from eating a rotten burrito?

If the acting was done well, and the story leading up to the last scene where the guy eats the burrito is engaging, then maybe. BUT THE LIKELIHOOD OF THAT HAPPENING IS SLIM.

Many of us may be living what appears to be a satisfying and meaningful life, but are actually quite meaningless. I know a gentleman who prided himself on his intuitive flair for spotting wigs. He considered this a tremendous virtue. Is his life meaningful?

> What about people who overindulge in sock puppets?

Or what about that guy who locked himself in a room, and died of his own farts? In the end, he died triumphantly, and with a clear conscience. But was he deluded? Only the devil knows for sure.

> DUDE, WHAT ABOUT US? What if our whole enterprise is meaningless? WHAT IF WE NEVER FIGURE OUT WHAT'S GOING ON? I mean, I was thinking. There is the Known and the unknown. And our whole quest is to Know the unknown. But once the unknown is uttered, doesn't it then become the Known?

You're right. We can't know the unknown because once we know the unknown, it becomes the known.

> Then it's true! Our goal to Know the unknown is utterly meaningless. AND OUR LIVES ARE MEANINGLESS.

Perhaps you're right.

> But wait, what if the unknown is uttered to some dude, but that dude was eating nachos at the time, and didn't hear it? Then is it still unknown?

I don't know.

> Then our mission still has hope.

REPLY FROM GUY

Mr. Jørgen Heinreckson
Nobel Prize Committee
The Nobel Institute
Boks 8072 Blindern
N-0288 Oslo
Norway

Trey Hamburger
681 Lake George Road
Leonard, MI 48367

Dear Mr. Hamburger:

Below, please find an answer in relation to a question
you sent to Mr. Jørgen Heinreckson of the Nobel
Foundation.

You wished, in your letter, to suggest that Trey
Hamburger be included among the candidates for the Nobel
Prize in Physics.

Our answer to your question is as follows:

By statute the right to submit a proposal for the
nomination of the Nobel Prize in Physics is reserved for
ONLY the following:

Members of the Royal Swedish Academy of Sciences;

Members of the Nobel Committee for Physics;

Professors of Physics at the universities and institutes
of technology of Finland, Iceland, Sweden, and Denmark,
as well as the Karolinska Institutet, Stockholm;

Past Nobel laureates in Physics;

One of the approximately three thousand individuals
invited by the Academy members to submit proposals

Any unsolicited proposals from a source not contained
in the above will be disqualified. *Self-nominations for the
Nobel Prize are disqualified.*

We hope this sufficiently answers your question and that
you appreciate our nomination rules. If your candidate is
properly evaluated, we will of course review him

Sincerely,
Mr. Jørgen Heinreckson
Secretary, the Nobel Assembly

40:
The Last Mission/
Facing Pure Evil

MIKE STEVENS AND I decide to withdraw our names from the Nobel Prize for Physics. It is a personal decision. We feel as though the Institution does not represent the needs of regular dudes—

—and the people who run it are dicks.

Regardless, I have before myself the Final Mission. I will go back to where this all started, back to Dead Derek's kitchen, and finally face this malevolent force. But I have to go ALONE.

PSYCHIC

THOUGHT

Pisces: in twenty minutes someone is going to offer you a chicken burger. **Take it.**

Dude.

Dude. Seriously. There comes a time in each man's existence where he has to face his destiny alone. I cannot allow you to follow me to my demise. This is a life or death or cheese-web situation. And it's our last chance to close the portal and stop everything that's been happening. You may come with me to Dead Derek's house, but you may not enter.

PURE EVIL

We walk over to Derek Wood's house real slow. I understand that Dead Derek's retarded dad may be there inside, waiting to strike. I remember the story about a friend of mine who signed up to be a camp counselor one summer. Turned out it was a camp for retarded people, which she didn't know about AT ALL until she got there. She said it was fun at first, with all the giggling and bubble blowing. That is, until a seemingly innocent spaghetti food fight turned REAL BAD REAL FAST. When she finally got home, she was covered with bite marks and still to this day, she won't speak a word of it to anyone.

And now, as I stand outside of Derek's dad's house, I may face a similar fate. But before I continue, I have to clear up ONE LAST THING. (It's the last time, *for real*.) Otherwise all of my accomplishments will be tarnished by this one brief oversight.

Did you know Hitler was an accomplished painter?

Few do. So here it goes. I know this is going to sound unbelievable after all of my many other misinterpreted instances of jerking off, but I have one last instance I need to clear up. Brian Trimmel, if you're reading this, I need to talk to you. *Seriously.* Do you remember yesterday when you were supposed to come to my house at 3:00 p.m. to pick up your brother's nunchakus, and you inconsiderately dropped by *ten minutes early*? You may remember coming down to the basement and seeing about $800 worth of porn violently strewn across the floor, and then seeing me innocently sitting between it all with my pants bunched up around my feet, *as if in a hurry*, and a handful of suntan lotion in my right hand. Do you remember that? Well, look, I know one's first impression would be that *Trey Hamburger is jerking off!* or *Trey Hamburger is about to jerk off!* And that would be understandable. But IT'S NOT TRUE, and there is a very good explanation. However, right now, I am not capable of providing you with that explanation. You are just going to have to trust me.

I can't defend you anymore.

Mike, you know me—

Dude, don't touch me.

COME ON MAN. YOU GOT TO BELIEVE ME! I WAS DOING SOMETHING TOTALLY DIFFERENT FROM WHAT YOU THINK I WAS DOING; BUT I AM NOT, at this moment, ABLE TO COME UP WITH AN EXPLANATION FOR WHAT THAT THING WAS!

...

Shit.

OK, well, whatever, with that finally off of my chest, I look toward Dead Derek Wood's house and the challenge that awaits. I start sauntering hard. I think about all the stuff that's happened. The "Indian"/Indian, the gurgling, the teleporting Hot Pockets, Derek evaporating, and I start getting really pissed off. Then I hear a ruffling in the bushes nearby. I bark furiously at the noise. It ceases immediately. I'm ready.

I don't know what/who I'm about to face in Derek's kitchen. I may have to fight a Hot Pocket, or it may give up and leave this dimension when it sees me running at it.

THE KITCHEN

I came to find Hot Pockets, and there's one. I look through the window, and I see the pastry on the kitchen table, chillin'. What's up, Motha Fucka. Yeah, we'll see. I walk around to the side door and slide it open real smooth. Before I enter, I stop for a moment. Can't let Derek's dad know I'm coming. Don't know if I can battle two entities at once. So I start sauntering quietly. I approach the kitchen and I can already feel the energy. The Hot Pocket is just sitting on a plate, acting like it doesn't give a shit, which fuels my anger. I form a psychic link with the entity and *the process of a psychic fight begins.* The Hot Pocket acknowledges my presence by exuding a puff of steam out of a combat symbiote. Immediately, its shields go up. My heart is getting attacked. It's going for my heart! A wise first move.

I focus on the Hot Pocket and begin my psychic cheese counterattack. It squeezes my brain, and my eyes pass before my life. I think of my fat neighbor bouncing in bed with his man titties flopping up and down. Then, out of nowhere, an unknown memory locked deep within my brain is released. The knowledge obtained during the beard/dimensional transference rushes toward the surface of my consciousness. I know what to do now.

I punch the Hot Pocket, and it explodes across the plate. *It is finished.*

I look up and Derek's retarded dad is pissed/hungry. And he goes right for my face. I cut the link with the Hot Pocket to protect myself from getting bit.

I'm able to twist and take Derek's dad onto the floor and we wrestle down there for a while. Then, when I'm about to get clawed up, Mike sticks his head through the window and yells, YO, STOP SCRATCHING MY AMIGO!

YO, STOP SCRATCHING MY AMIGO!

And Mike chucks a hypnotized duck through the window and it hits Derek's dad HARD. This gives me enough of a distraction that I can scratch *his* face and escape out the front door. I am not proud of myself at this very moment, but I survive.

Sorry about presuming you were jerking off when you were surrounded by 1800 of porn violently strewn across the carpet.

Don't worry about it.

No, seriously. Amigos should support amigos even when an amigo's pants are clumsily bunched up around their ankles and they have a hand full of suntan lotion.

Thanks. Now let's just move on.

After Mike and I defeat the entity and reconcile, we walk out of Derek's driveway, and then, out of nowhere, WE SEE DEREK WOOD, JUST STANDING THERE. ALIVE.

PSYCHIC THOUGHT

Pisces: I know I told you that if someone offers you a chicken burger, then you should take it. Please disregard that advice. It may be the last chicken burger you ever eat.

41:

Shit, the Apocalypse

OK, Derek Wood introduces to us some knowledge that pretty much makes our whole investigation meaningless/ retarded. That gurgling sound that has been ruling our lives for the past week—it was Jeff Trenton THE WHOLE TIME. *He's got rabies.*

On an emotional level, I'm pissed.

Derek tells me that seven days ago, Jeff stuck his head in a hole in a tree, and a squirrel bit up his face over twelve times.

The initial phase of his rabies started when he whaled on his neighbor over that Cabo Chicken Sub. He was no longer afraid of other mammalia whether it be bear or human. Then came the gurgling. Every time we heard the gurgle and spilled our potato chips and pop, it was just Jeff Trenton flipping out in the woods, hunting for food.

So the whole story he told us about Derek getting vaporized was basically bullshit. Jeff just wanted our burritos. And his rabid mind would stop at nothing to achieve those burritos, *even if it meant lying to a dude you've know for over three years.* The problem was that we could never verify Derek's fate because his retarded dad doesn't speak English.

He chirps.

Derek tells us that he was at his grandpa's the whole time, chillin'.

So I got a bikini wax for nothing!

I'm afraid so. And Jeff really isn't a textbook anal sadist after all.

All that psychoanalysis meant nothing! He's just a regular guy who put himself in the position of having his face bitten by a squirrel over twelve times!

But, dude, when I fought that Hot Pocket, I felt something. Something was actually psychically fighting back and attacking my heart. And what about the really old guy with the flipper scratch? He saw something, didn't he?

Old people don't know what's going on most of the time. Last month me and Josh Marshall were driving through Ohio when we saw this old fucker in an ELECTRIC WHEELCHAIR going down the freeway with a cigarette hanging out of his mouth. He was going maybe 12 mph in the right lane. Fucking crazy. Everybody was honking and flashing their lights, and the guy just kept on rolling. I totally respect that shit, but DAMN.

That old codger. This means everything we've been working toward was BULLSHIT/ABSURD. THEN WHAT'S THE POINT OF OUR LIVES?

WARNING:

IF SOMEBODY YOU KNOW GETS RABIES:

* Don't listen to him.

* Get him out of your house.

* Call his mom.

* While waiting for mom, give him a paper towel to wipe the wound.

And here it is,
The End of the World.
Things will be different now.
So I go to the meatball factory and
take off my pants,
sit in the pond nearby,
and evaporate.

Thomas Siebold
Office 711
Kedzi Hall
18 University Hill Drive
Oppenheimer University
Holly, MI 48442

Trey Hamburger
681 Lake George Road
Leonard, MI 48367

September 28, 2008

Dear Mr. Trey Hamburger, Scientist,

I have received your letter regarding the existence of extraterrestrials and ghosts and I have found it very intriguing. I am excited about your thirst for knowledge! As I am trained in chemistry, I am no expert in extraterrestrials or ghostly matters. So I can only give you my opinion for what it's worth. If we were to calculate the probability that there exists life elsewhere in the universe, you may be surprised at the results. A radio astronomer named Frank Drake created an equation that roughly calculates the number of potential technically advanced civilizations in our galaxy. He did this by multiplying the following factors:

the number of stars in our galaxy (approximately 100 billion) times

the fraction of stars that have planets (50 percent of stars have planets) times

the average number of planets that could support life per star (2 per star, approximately) times

the fraction of the above planets where life could evolve (100 percent of planets that can support life will have life evolved on it) times

the fraction of the above planets where intelligence could evolve (about 1 percent of the above planets will have intelligent life) times

the fraction of the above planets that could communicate (1 percent of those will be able to communicate) times

the amount of time the civilizations that could communicate survive (scientists estimate that to be 10,000 years)

The resulting number is around ten civilizations. Although the exact figures for many of these factors are unknown, they were calculated by very smart people!

Now that's just our galaxy. There are over 100 billion
galaxies in our Universe. So, as a scientific authority
(not of astrophysics though!), I think I can safely say
the likelihood that advanced life exists outside of Earth
is nearly certain!

The whole world is full of mysteries such as this, and
I hope this encourages you to continue your intellectual
journey wherever it takes you!

If you have any other questions, or would like to
discuss any other scientific matters further, feel free
to contact me. I always enjoy speaking with people who
are curious and are willing to pursue their passions no
matter how different they may be!

My e-mail is tungston53@oppenheimer.edu

Sincerely,
Thomas Siebold

Dude, this guy actually thinks that there is stuff that
doesn't exist that really does exist.

No way.

NATIONAL FEDERATION OF RETARDED PEOPLE
Okalahoma

NFRP
1234 Retard Road
Stupid Idiot, OK 47362924

Thomas Siebold
Office 711
Kedzi Hall
18 University Hill Drive
Oppenheimer University
Holly, MI 48442

Dear Thomas,

Congratulations, YOU'RE IN.

Salutations,

Trey Hamburger, NOT the president

Trey Hamburger

Mike Stevens, also NOT the president

MIKE STEVENS

THE END[34]

EXHIBITS
AND SECRETS

EXHIBIT A

Few know this, but the potato chip was invented out of spite. At this one restaurant in 1853, a customer named Cornelius Vanderbilt started bitching about his French fries being *too thick.* (Who does that?) So the chef, a man by the name of George Crum, was like, *Oh yeah, motherfucker, how about I cut some fries that are THIN AS FUCK.* So as the waiter brought out the "fries," Mr. Crum watched behind a silky translucent curtain. And guess what, Cornelius Vanderbilt loved it, and now potato chips are second in human consumption only to water.

I will fuck up your meal.

George Crum, the inventor of
the Potato Chip

Commodore Cornelius Vanderbilt,
the guy that complained about
the fries

And I will love it.

The next week however, another customer came in and bitched about the chicken. Crum then made the guy a plate of sautéed chicken, smothered in marinara and bacon, oozing with Monterey Jack cheese, and DRIZZLED WITH PUBES. Fortunately the meal never caught on.

EXHIBIT B

IMPORTANT NOTE FOR SCIENTIFIC OFFICIALS: _TREY HAMBURGER WOULD NEVER EAT DICK-SHAPED CRACKERS_

I'm not a gay. **Item 1:** I've had sex with a forty-year-old naked bitch when I was kickin' it down at Daytona Beach with my cousin and my two best friends, and, surprisingly, ended up having a really wonderful evening. **Item 2:** In August, I went to a relative's house and there was a cat there and I picked it up and started petting it and shit and the cat was cool. And one of the ladies eating lunch turned and said, "Looks like Sebastian has made a new friend." And I was like, "Isn't Sebastian a man's name?" And the lady was like, "SURE IS—THAT CAT IS A MAN." I IMMEDIATELY ceased petting. **Item 3:** On the Discovery Channel there were these two plants and each of them was a male species plant, and I was cool with it at first. But then, the announcer started saying that they were about to exchange pollen. I was like, Shit. The next morning my mom busts into my room asking why the garden was all torn apart. I told her to get out of my face.

I'm sorry I had to put it so bluntly, but after certain parties saw me eating quiche, which was WHAT MY MOM HAPPENED TO MAKE FOR LUNCH THAT AFTERNOON YOU FUCKING ASSHOLE, and those certain parties said certain things to certain people, I thought it necessary to clear up this matter. Plus, I don't want to pick up the phone expecting a scientist to be calling about facts and experiments and it ends up being some sweaty dude calling about dicks and feelings. With that being said, I will not address this matter again. Also, please understand that I don't have any problems with gay people.

Using gay as a derogatory term is gay.

EXHIBIT C:
*A Seemingly Innocuous Document from One
Colonel to Another*

WARNING: This is a TOP-SECRET-EYES ONLY document containing
the highest level of secret documents imaginable.

November 18, 1985

██
██
████████ blankets just started going nuts. ████
██
████████████████████████████████████ puked. ███
████████████████

Colonel ████████ *don't show this to anybody.* Seriously.

Thanks a lot,
Colonel ████████

EXHIBIT D:

Alien Abduction Test

Coming to believe that you've been abducted by aliens is a gradual process. First you find your pajama top unbuttoned during the night, and then . . .

* You ever woken up in the middle of the night and felt like a suction cup was just caressing your head?
* You ever been watching TV and then out of nowhere, it's way later than you thought it was, like the time went *missing*?
* Do you sometimes, while doing something totally unrelated to spaceships and space, all of a sudden just start thinking about spaceships and space?
* Have you ever had images or memories of getting a backrub by a flipper?
* Do you frequently feel like someone is being watched by you?
* For the ladies: Have any of your fetuses disappeared without a trace?
* Do you want to be near aliens?
* Do you like watching movies about aliens, but you can't help yourself from thinking that they have a specific part totally wrong?
* You ever seen some weird-ass fog?
* Have you ever felt like you can't commit to a long-term relationship because you have this feeling that you might not be spending much more time in this galaxy?
* Do you have trouble trusting hairless people?

If you answered yes to three or more of these questions, you need to talk to a buddy NOW.

EXHIBIT E:

Suggested Workout Schedule

Daily Schedule:

6:00 a.m.	Wake up + Push-ups
7:00 a.m.	Push-ups
8:00 a.m.	Push-ups
9:00 a.m.	Protein shake + crunches
10:00 a.m.	Push-ups
11:00 a.m.	Push-ups
12:00 p.m.	Push-ups
1:00 p.m.	Protein shake + crunches
2:00 p.m.	Push-ups
3:00 p.m.	Push-ups
4:00 p.m.	Push-ups
5:00 p.m.	Push-ups
6:00 p.m.	Push-ups
7:00 p.m.	Push-ups
8:00 p.m.	Push-ups
9:00 p.m.	Shower + push-ups
10:00 p.m.	Push-ups
11:00 p.m.	Brush teeth + push-ups
12:00 a.m.	Bed + push-ups
1:00 a.m.	Onwards Sleep + Push-ups + Intravenous Protein Shake + Chill

Using this schedule, I have worked out every day for the last day.

EXHIBIT F:

Elite Fighting Force Starter Manual

CREATING AN ELITE FIGHTING FORCE OF REALLY INTENSE DUDES

Field Guide by Mike Stevens

All right motherfuckers, are you ready for some heavy shit? If you know other people around your neighborhood who think like you do, and wouldn't feel ashamed wearing a motorcycle helmet and running down the street swinging around nunchakus, then give them this leaflet too. We'd like to coordinate efforts.

OK, before you let anybody to join your Elite Fighting Force, make each applicant sign a nondisclosure agreement informing them of the consequences if they can't keep their mouths shut. And before training, the applicant must then sign a final document declaring his/her allegiance to the unit.

Below is a list of the some of the necessary operational roles needed.

OPERATIONAL ROLES

Medic
Sniper(s)
Demolitions expert
Hypnotist
Kickboxers
Cryptologist
Computer genius
Ninjas (part time/full time)
Francophone/Language expert with some fighting skill and
    Stealth Mode training
Anybody with a machine gun or Uzi
Anybody who has $1,000 and doesn't care what happens to it

Once established, this group of people will make up a covert organization with extremely tight security. With enough money and connections, the organization could have motherfucking satellites zipping around shooting lasers, ramming into suspicious crafts, and taking geospatial pictures of butt naked ladies.

PREREQUISITES FOR JOINING OUR TEAM

No previous courtmartial convictions: We need people who
will listen to the mission commander. *When he says kill,
members must kill.*

Mental stability: Don't want anybody running if they hear
something weird.

Stamina: Pass a 100 meter sprint test while wearing a
full suit of armor and/or covered in blankets—self
explanatory.

Spontaneous: Willing to go ape shit if there's danger or make
a bad-ass logo if we need a new one right away.

Miscellaneous: Must be able to manipulate animal (bird or
mammal) without saying a word. (Don't worry, this will
all be made clear later.)

And we will have our own radar equipment to detect
weird shit and have mobile units which could basically
go anywhere in the contiguous United States and initiate
capture and ass-beating protocols. Each unit could be
equipped with the latest in high-tech laser weaponry and
machine guns with several katana swords.

Motherfucking MP-5 machine gun with infrared laser
sights, *perfect for close-quarter battle*

QUESTIONS AND ANSWERS

WHAT CAN YOU EXPECT FROM THE UNIT?

• Execution of plans that are the culmination of ideas
  spawned ten minutes earlier

• Being around a group of dudes who are the most intense
  people you'll ever meet, and that's a fact

• Making love to some of the most beautiful women on the
  planet

• Firing a crossbow from the passenger side of a moving
  car

• Horseback riding

• Swimming

• Shooting live targets

As for the unit itself, the members of the team would
be few, but specialized and trustworthy. There would be
twenty-five employed, and each would be checked through a

rigorous background evaluation and a process of intense questioning to filter out the potential talkers. Of course after the initial phase, there will be a battery of psychological tests so that we can keep out any psychopathic killers or people who would lose it if somebody made a joke, which shouldn't be a big deal, but the guy can't stop thinking about it, when he should really just let it go. Finally there will be a loyalty test of allowing a preapproved member shoot an arrow at the applicant.

WHAT DOES THE TRAINING CONSIST OF?

- Go down to Mexico; get into a bunch of fights; leave
- Laser Weaponry Practice if we get some lasers
- Getting pumped up and punching trees
- That's all right now

WILL I GET A CHANCE TO KILL?
Yes.

CAN MY GIRLFRIEND HANG OUT DURING THE TRAINING SESSIONS?
No way.

Only the central commanders, Trey and I, would know the identity of all employees. Each unit will have its own quadrant, but will know nothing about what the other dudes are doing. Each unit will think they are the ONLY unit. All members would be hired in some classified advertisement to do something "intense."

Each member would communicate over secure channels via e-mail, *never phone*. To keep the secrecy at the highest level possible, seventeen front companies would be set up. No matter what, members working at each front company could never meet a member from another unit. So for example, any two front companies CANNOT be in the exact same business. For example, mattress sales. This may lead to an accidental compromise of secrecy when one dude notices that another dude at a similar front company is getting all weird when they're trying to do fake business together.

So if you are a U.S. citizen and you are interested in guns and squatting in your rucksacks as fucking helicopters are landing ten feet away AND have a firm dislike of ghosts/aliens, then you are a perfect candidate. If you succeed in demonstrating your ability, then you can join up. It's your call.

Mike Stevens
Elite Fighting Force of Really Intense Dudes, Central Commander B

EXHIBIT G:

Correspondence with the CERN

Trey Hamburger
681 Lake George Road
Leonard, MI 48367

CERN Visits Service
Mailbox CO9600
CH 1211 Genève 23
Switzerland

March 13, 2008

Dear CERN,

Mike Stevens and I have decided to become Pure Energy.
  It took us a long time to come to that conclusion, and
ten minutes after Mike thought of it out of nowhere, it
has become a necessary step in our ghosts/aliens plan.
  Me, my associate Mike Stevens, and his uncle will be in
Geneva from the period of October 21 to October 29, 2008,
and we would very much like to visit the CERN. We are
very excited to see the largest particle accelerator in
the world.
  Now, we have a very important question and I want you to
think about this before you come to an answer. Is there a
chance Mike and I could get inside the machine itself and
have particles fired at us? At first you may be thinking
No way. But what if we offered to sign a waiver that
basically states that we totally wanted to do it, and we
won't come after you in court? I'll have a lawyer write up
some paperwork that takes the legal responsibility out of
your hands. You won't have to worry about *anything*. This
is our choice. Our goal is to open up a portal to another
dimension, and this could be the only way.
  Thank you for your time, and I hope to be hearing your
response soon. Mike and I will be welding armor for our
voyage in the meantime.

See you soon,
Trey Hamburger

Trey Hamburger

Mike Stevens,

MIKE STEVENS

CERN Visits Service
Mailbox CO9600
CH 1211 Genève 23
Switzerland
tel. +41 22 767 █████
fax. +41 22 767 █████

Mr. Trey Hamburger,

Your letter was received 27 March.
   This letter is NOT a confirmation of your visit for the
dates of 21-29 October 2008.
   We appreciate your enthusiasm for visiting the CERN.
Public visits to the CERN are free of charge. However,
anyone under ten years old will not be admitted.
   Visits to the CERN are organised for groups of twelve
or more at a minimum. The maximum is fifty people. The
languages available for each group are English, German,
French, and Italian. Each visit includes an introductory
talk, a short film about the CERN, a tour of two sites at
the CERN, and finally the Microcosm exhibition.
   For the period of January through July and October
through November, a one-year advanced booking for visits
is required.
   Unfortunately, due to the high number of requests to
visit, we will have to decline your request for a visit.
However, you can book a visit for 2009, as many of our
dates are free.
   We also regret to inform you that we cannot allow
visitors to get inside the accelerator and have particles
shot at them. Due to the liability and ethical problems
of any injuries that a visitor could sustain, even if
that visitor signs a waiver, we cannot fulfill your
request. Please call our Visits Service Center tel. +41
22 767 █████ or view our website at outreach.web.cern.
ch/outreach/en/Visits/Info-en.html if you have any more
inquires.

Thank you,
Michelle Battajon
CERN Visits Center

I don't think we could have gotten over there anyway.

EXHIBIT H:

Letter to Nabisco

Trey Hamburger
681 Lake George Road
Leonard, MI 48367

Kraft Food
Nabisco
Global Corporate Headquarters
Three Lakes Drive
Northfield, IL 60093

Dear Nabisco,

I'm an avid fan of crackers. When people come over to
my house they know that they'll be eating crackers. My
favorite brand is Nabisco.
   Which is why I was shocked when I found out that
Nabisco has the copyright to building a UFO. I have two
questions: How did you get that information? And don't
you think it should be available to everyone?
   Other than that minor hiccup, I am very pleased with
your products.

Thank you,
Trey Hamburger

P.S. If you guys are thinking about making any dick-
shaped products, I will no longer advocate your crackers.

NO REPLY . . .

By neither denying nor
acknowledging our claim, they may be
protecting themselves from making a false
testimony.

Or maybe the organization is so compartmentalized that no one
individual really knows everything there is to know.

EXHIBIT I:

Letter to Some Dude

Trey Hamburger
681 Lake George Road
Leonard, MI 48367

Professor Jack Mckinzie
Physics Department, University of Michigan
61123 Randall Laboratory
450 Church Street
Ann Arbor, MI 48109-1040

Dear Professor Jack Mckinzie,

CONGRADUATIONS!

The Society for Scientific Progress cordially invites you to a colloquium debate on December 14, 2008, at Todd "Semen" Niemen's house. It's pretty much going to be a few of us there, hanging out.

What I'm thinking is that you and I could meet earlier, maybe at Burger King, and then drive over to Todd's together. And then at the party, I'd bring up a point and motion to you, like scratch my face or something, and you'll start saying all these facts to support it, and everybody else will be like, "Wow, sorry, Trey." But you'll keep going because you'll be all eloquent and shit and I'll be just sitting back chillin', acting like I was above the whole thing, but still recognizing that my points are sufficiently proven.

You'll probably be the oldest guy there by forty years, so nobody is going to be much of a challenge in the debate. So don't worry. The only condition is that you're on my side *because I brought you*. If you end up proving me wrong ABOUT ANYTHING, I don't know, but that's something that really upsets me, you'll have to get your own ride home.

Note, before we meet up, please pick up two bottles of peppermint Schnapps and a bottle of Jägermeister and whatever you want for yourself.

Peace,
Trey Hamburger, Colloquium Director
Society for Scientific Progress

P.S. Please bring your résumé and/or your degree from Harvard for references. Todd "Semen" Niemen is definitely going to ask for it. I know it.

NO REPLY

Guidelines for Scientific
Argumentation
     1) Focus on your disputant's claims.
     Do their conclusions follow from
     their premises? If not, use logic and
     evidence to show otherwise.
If 1) fails,
     B) Start punching.

INITIATION FORM

ELITE FIGHTING FORCE OF REALLY INTENSE DUDES
Est. a couple weeks ago

I, [name in CAPITAL LETTERS here] , am cool, and promise to become a member of the Elite Fighting Force.[35]

Check box if you're totally serious. ☐

---

[35]If you don't want to join up, then please fill out the following form on the next page.

NATIONAL FEDERATION OF RETARDED PEOPLE

EST. 1986

This is to certify that

___[your name in CAPITAL LETTERS here]___ has been awarded the
Certificate of Retardedness for his/her work in furthering the
field of being retarded.

Served,

Trey Hamburger, Not the President

Trey Hamburger

Mike Stevens, Not the President *Either*

MIKE STEVENS

SUPPORT GROUPS

Yeast Infection Support Groups

Natural Healing Support Group
26 Brittany Drive
Asheville, NC 28804

REAL Women Solution
1093 East Hemingway
Clarkston, CT 06019

INVESTIGATION NOTES

NOBODY KNOWS.

PRECISELY

NUMCHUCKS must be...

THE CONSTANT

Are we really ourselves?

I DON'T KNOW

Once my mission here is complete, I'll definitely be moving on to the next plane and chill'n the FUCK OUT

Who runs the NFL?

PLEASE DO NOT CLOSE YOUR MIND TO THIS STUFF.

PROCTOR & GAMBLE & SATAN

ME TOO!

Pine

Tree

...is virtually FLAT I'VE NOTICED

A DUCK'S QUACK DOESN'T ECHO, AND NO ONE KNOWS WHY

NOBODY KNOWS

Surveillance

commonly found between CHICKEN TOES.

THERE IS BAD SHIT HAPPENING ALL OVER THE GLOBE. it happens long before you...

EXPLOSIONS

THESE DAMNED THESIS

Do you have any ... to happen in 2012?

DID I REALLY JUST HAVE A CONVERSATION WITH A BIRD?

what the hell going on at these labs?

I DON'T KNOW

IGNORANT

BONELESS BUFFALO WINGS

IN CASE THE GOVERNMENT DOES TRY TO DO SOMETHING CRAZY

build a

Kill him with pepperonis

Usually if some dude were to say that shit to me, I ... BIG WHOOP. But he said it like he meant it. So I was like SHIT.

MORE INVESTIGATION NOTES

ou see that maker sense. I've heard way to many quotes from Plato/Hecules, etc. that make No sense.

DON'T TALK ABOUT THIS TO ANYONE ELSE.

ALSO, I'D FLIP OUT AND THEM, DEAD, I Prbbly would too.

SOMEBODY TOLD ME I WERE if I WATZE A GHOST AND

ude, this may don't think mankind is we seriously truly for ETs tomorrow, maybe essed us I ready for a few hundred years from now, but not this week.

they say everyone has different finger print, but who knows, they can't check every bodies

PLUTO's CONJUNCTION WITH THE GALACTIC CENTER OCCURS ONCE EVERY 248 YEARS

I MENTIONED THIS TO AN ALLY AND HE AGREED

A NEW WOULD

PISS ANYBODY

OFF.

-IFE for

None of this H can be

TO PERCEPTUALISE.

ITS EXTREMELY HARD WITH

MY 5 MACHINE

INFRARED LASER

SHE'S PERFECT

CEREBRAL THOUGHTS FOR CEREBRAL PEOPLE

bad bend with

AnyWAYS.

Twisted Subbed Today

MORTAL VS NON-MORTAL REALM

I wonder what if your head could break down and your whole world just vanish

like if there is a chance that the molecular in

Very weird villian in a billion

elephant skin things with lobster like claws.

GOOD

NO. is IT? GIVES YOU A REWARD FIRST.

Check the reward POLICE MIGHT INVOLVED

explain it. Save up enough money, quit your job sell your car, start roaming the EARTH until you find it.

If this fails and we can't think of anything e well will bring th close and blow up th planet.

Jet some

, Keme Sabe, we'll

FOR

You far or against uper Rifles?

WHEN DEALING WITH SHIFTERS, USE ICE

IS THIS ONE OF IT THOSE PREDICAMATIC PHILOSOPHICAL QUESTIONS THAT REQUIRES US TO KNOW OURSELVES BEFORE WE CAN ANSWER

ABOUT THE AUTHORS AND ANOTHER GUY WE KNOW

Trey Hamburger (Author and Central Commander Class A/Earl)

Personal camouflage and concealment skills (can hide from hunter forces)
High running speeds
Familiar with the broadsword.
Crossbow training
Leadership potential
Well-trained in aquatic/semiaquatic terrain
Hates the government
Has worked in retail

Mike Stevens (Back-up Author/Amigo and Central Commander Class B)
Knows the effects of various chemicals and biological agents and how to spot symptoms of them in others
Martial arts trained in swords, knives, blunt weapons, and some hand-to-hand styles
Studied the weak points of the body vigorously
Ambush tactics
Sometimes wishes his best friend was a unicorn.
Escape and evasion
Projectile throwing (shuriken *multi point and single point*)
Certified vagina expert

Jeff Trenton (Part of the Elite Fighting Force, But Not an Author and Definitely Not a Central Commander)
Escape and evasion expert
Sniper training
Could eat a person if stuck somewhere
Knows how to fight to kill only (incapable of any fake fighting because he *doesn't want amigos dead*)
Extremely close to joining his mind and body into a single weapon
Completed Red Cross Lifeguard Training last summer
Does not have the powerful gift of chi but wants it badly